Two more men charged up the hill and Horgan realized with a shock that one of them was Hansen. The minister's face was a contorted mask of hatred as he rushed toward Horgan, and the scout reached out to grab him around the ankles. The minister fell heavily to the ground, losing his white-knuckled grip on his rifle.

Hansen screamed like a banshee, then whirled on Horgan. "You damned idiot! What are you trying to do?"

"I'm trying to save your life, and Mrs. Hansen's in the bargain," Horgan said, unclenching his teeth just long enough to get the words out.

Hansen snorted, his teeth bared like fangs, then scrambled free from Horgan's grasp. He got to his feet, his head swiveling wildly as he looked for his weapon.

"You damned fool," Horgan hissed. "You'll get your wife killed!"

"The only way to save her is to get her out of here," Hansen said, panting. "And that's just what I intend to do."

Whirling, he plunged on down the hill, leaving Horgan to call after him, "Come back, damn you. Come back before it's too late."

Also by Bill Dugan

Duel on the Mesa
Texas Drive
Gun Play at Cross Creek
Brady's Law

War Chiefs
Geronimo
Chief Joseph
Crazy Horse
Quanah Parker
Sitting Bull

Published by
HarperPaperbacks

ATTENTION: ORGANIZATIONS AND CORPORATIONS

Most HarperPaperbacks are available at special quantity discounts for bulk purchases for sales promotions, premiums, or fund-raising. For information, please call or write:
Special Markets Department, HarperCollins Publishers,
10 East 53rd Street, New York, N.Y. 10022.
Telephone: (212) 207-7528. Fax: (212) 207-7222.

DEATH SONG

BILL DUGAN

HarperPaperbacks
A Division of HarperCollins*Publishers*

This is a work of fiction. The characters, incidents, and
dialogues are products of the author's imagination and are
not to be construed as real. Any resemblance to actual events
or persons, living or dead, is entirely coincidental.

HarperPaperbacks   *A Division of* HarperCollins*Publishers*
10 East 53rd Street, New York, N.Y. 10022

Cover illustration by Bill Dodge

First printing: June 1994

Printed in the United States of America

HarperPaperbacks and colophon are trademarks of
HarperCollins*Publishers*

❖ 10 9 8 7 6 5 4 3 2 1

Johm Hansen looked at himself in the mirror. He felt uncomfortable in the denim shirt and jeans. More used to the stiff formality of his black suit, he barely recognized himself in the glass. He wondered if anyone in his congregation would recognize him now. The blond hair was the same, the mustache a little darker, the same razor glow on his cheeks, but he didn't look much like a man of the cloth. And because he didn't look like one, he didn't feel like one.

He leaned closer, trying to see into the depths of his eyes, where the watery blue shifted as if wracked by hidden currents. He realized that it was appearance, as much as anything else, that gave a man his station, especially in a community of strangers. Look like a bum, you'll be treated like one. Proper, that's what he wanted to be, and he wasn't convinced it was proper for a Presbyterian minister to be traipsing off into the hills on a picnic. But Susan had insisted, and he always did what Susan wanted.

He could see her in the mirror, fussing with her hair. She had wanted to wear jeans, too, but John had drawn the line at that. That was a breach of etiquette he could not tolerate. "It would look bad," he insisted, and Susan, knowing how desperate he was to make a good impression on his new flock, had acquiesced, but not without a good-natured fight.

There were times when he thought that perhaps Susan was too wild for him. Nothing seemed capable of repressing her spirit, even when decorum was at risk. Watching her now, standing there in her chemise, combing her hair with a pleasure that was almost obscene, he couldn't help but wonder if maybe she was too beautiful for him, too beautiful to be a minister's wife. She was nothing like the wives of his professors at the seminary, women who seemed so stiff they could have been made of pressed paper. Where those women had pinched faces and cold eyes, Susan had a ready smile. Her cheeks were round, soft, pink, not the fishbelly white parchment of the older wives.

Dr. Alderson had spoken to him once about Susan, saying she had "a lot of spunk." But John knew that his mentor regarded spunk as something less than desirable, especially in a minister's wife. There were times when he wondered why Susan had married him in the first place. They seemed so different. She was so alive that he would find himself occasionally thinking that she was some other species altogether. It wasn't that

she did not respect what he did. She was virtu-
ous, if not devout, but it seemed sometimes that
there was so much life in her it couldn't help but
bubble out of her, like water in a hot spring, and
that there was nothing she could do to prevent it.

He tugged on his shirt, hitched up his jeans,
and turned to face her. She smiled while the
brush hissed through her long brown hair.
"There," she said, "doesn't that feel more comfortable?"

Hansen smiled back and felt that his cheeks
were a little too tight for the expression, as if it
was artificial, and, he reflected, perhaps it was. "I
feel a little silly," he answered.

Susan laughed, and her eyes sparkled. "Not
silly. You just feel human, John. It'll be good for
you. You're so hard on yourself. Sometimes I
think maybe you're afraid to relax. But nobody
will think any the less of you, or your calling, if
you allow yourself to have some fun once in a
while. In fact, I think people will like you all the
more for it. It'll make them feel more at ease.
People don't want to feel like they have to walk
on eggs around their minister."

Hansen tried another smile, and this time it
seemed to work a little better. "In my head, I
know you're right, Susan," he said. "But in here,"
he said, tapping his chest with a rigid finger, "I'm
not so sure."

Putting her hairbrush on the dresser, she
reached for her dress and pulled it over her head,
tugging it down to hug her hips. It caught on her
ample breasts for a moment, pushing them out,
and he felt himself blush. When the dress was

finally down, she spun in a graceful pirouette. "How do I look?" she asked.

"Pretty as a picture. Just like always."

"You just say that because you're supposed to." She walked toward him, her arms out. He took her hands, squeezed them, and stiffened as she leaned forward to peck him on the tip of his nose. "We'll have a nice time, John. You'll see. You've been working too hard. It'll do you good to spend time away from your work."

He nodded. "I know you're right. You usually are. I guess I'm just too proper, too . . . stuffy."

"You are that," she said, softening the truth with a radiant smile. "You have to learn to let people see what's inside you. Don't keep such a tight rein on your feelings, John. It's not good for you."

Hansen was getting uncomfortable. Even the loose collar of the denim shirt seemed to hamper his breathing, and he tucked a couple of fingers inside to stretch it a bit. "I have to get the wagon ready," he said. "I'll wait for you outside."

"I won't be long. Lunch is already made."

He left the room, glancing backward at his wife as she fastened the last buttons of her bodice. She stuck out her tongue and wrinkled her nose at him as he pulled the door closed.

Outside, under the bright sun, he walked to the corral, brought the horses out one at a time, and hitched them to the buckboard. He thought once more how he wished he was more comfortable in the saddle. Susan rode so easily, even brilliantly, taking to the western saddle like a duck to water, but he always felt as if the horse were about to leave him behind. He worked at it, too hard, Susan kept telling him. "You have to relax, let the horse relax, John. You're making him nervous."

But try as he might, he never seemed to get the hang of it. Occasionally, he would visit a sick congregant on horseback, but whenever he and Susan went someplace together, they used the wagon. She teased him that he was embarrassed because she rode better than he did. He laughed it off, but knew there was more than a little truth to what she said. Colorado was every bit as beautiful as they'd been told, but it was an alien world for him.

Within a week of his arrival in Chandler, he had wanted to turn around and go back home, find a church somewhere in the East, someplace civilized. But Susan had fallen instantly in love with the mountains, and by the end of their first week, he knew it would break her heart to leave them behind. He kept telling himself that he would adjust, that it was just a matter of time. A year later, he was still telling himself the same thing, and it seemed no closer to coming true than it had that first week. He still felt like a complete stranger, and was beginning to believe that he always would.

When the team was hitched, he climbed aboard, jerked the reins, and brought the wagon to the house, where he set the brake and climbed down. Susan was already closing the door, a wicker hamper balanced on one hip. Hansen climbed to the porch, took the picnic hamper, and leaned over to set it in the back of the wagon. Then he went inside and came back out with his rifle, a

Winchester repeater that he had fired once or twice, telling himself that it was practice.

Susan climbed up into the seat, defeating his intention of a gallant hoist. He circled around back and climbed into the driver's seat, released the brake, and clucked to the team as he snapped the reins. "Not as nice as a coach and four, milady, but 'twill have to serve."

Susan laughed, a throaty sound that never failed to amuse him. As the house fell away behind them, she kept looking back over her shoulder. "It's so pretty here, John. I'm really glad we came, aren't you?"

He wasn't, at least not as glad as she, and she knew it, but she hadn't given up trying to convince him of their good fortune in getting so beautiful a setting for his first ministry.

The team settled into a leisurely gait, and he was content to let them have their head. It was enough to be on the seat beside her, to see her radiant smiles as she watched the birds and nearly swooned over the imposing serenity of the mountains towering far ahead of them, their peaks still covered with snow, their slopes dark green and slate gray in the brilliant sunlight.

"Anyplace in particular you'd care to go, Sue?" he asked.

"Yes. How about that little glade we found last month, on Miller's Creek?"

"It's kind of far, isn't it?"

"Not that far. And it's so pretty there. So peaceful. It's perfect for a picnic."

He bobbed his head and snapped the reins to prod the horses into a little more speed. Susan, as usual, was content to ride in silence, and he rather enjoyed the quiet, so they spoke hardly at all until the first glitter of Miller's Creek came into view as they broke over the crest of a hill nearly an hour later.

Hansen let the horses settle down again and rode with one hand on the brake handle. Susan teased him about being afraid of getting anywhere in too much of a hurry, and he laughed, but still kept the brake within easy reach.

Fifteen minutes later, the road bottomed out, and the creek was little more than a quarter-mile away. They closed on the creek bed, where the road ran parallel for nearly a mile before reaching Miller's Bridge.

But they wouldn't have to go that far. The glade Susan had chosen was just a few hundred yards away, at a point where the road curved away from the water for a bit to circle the base of a low hill. Hansen pulled the wagon off the road and into the tall grass, set the brake, and looped the reins around the brake handle. By the time he was finished, Susan was already on the ground, the hamper wrapped in her arms.

He took it from her and hoisted it to his right shoulder, then followed his wife, who was skipping like a schoolgirl ahead of him through the lush green. Her chosen spot was surrounded by willows and cottonwoods, shielded from the road, and filled with the babble of the creek, where it dropped a few feet over stones, foamed away from the deep pool, then grew quiet again.

Nearly a hundred yards ahead of him now, she swept the willow branches aside with a theatrical flourish, then disappeared behind them like an actress waiting for one more curtain call.

He stopped for a moment to catch his breath, then pushed on. He was still thirty yards from the willows when he heard a shrill yelp that seemed cut off before it was finished. "Sue?" he called. "Are you all right?"

There was no answer. He stopped then, uncertain. "Susan, stop fooling, now."

But still there was no answer. Sensing that something was wrong, he dropped the hamper and started to run toward the willows. "Susan? Are you all right? Susan?"

He heard another shriek, and it took him a moment to realize that she was calling his name. "Joooohhhnnnn!"

He reached the willows just in time to hear a splash as someone crossed the creek. He pushed on through the thick branches in time to see Susan draped over a spotted horse, its reins clutched in the fist of an Indian warrior who had a bow slung across his back. Just ahead of him two more warriors, their heads turned toward Hansen to reveal their brightly painted faces, grinned at him. A moment later, they vanished through willows on the far side of the creek.

He cursed himself for having left his rifle in the wagon, and didn't know whether to run back for it or to race on across the water unarmed. For a moment, he did neither, then he splashed across the shallow stream and screamed at the top of his lungs, "Susan?"

He was careening headlong toward the trees when the curtain of willows parted and one of the three Indians thundered toward him, a rifle held by the barrel brandished high overhead. He saw the arc of the descending rifle butt and tried to ward it off, but he lost his balance and managed to break but not avoid the crash of the wooden stock that glanced off his temple and sent him to his knees as everything turned black around him.

Hansen heard the burble of the creek before he opened his eyes. An ant crawled across his cheek, and as he reached to brush it away, his fingers felt the sticky ooze of blood from his temple. When he opened his eyes, he saw patches of sunlight on the grass. Trying to sit up, he had the sensation of the earth spinning beneath him. His head throbbed, and he wondered whether his skull had been fractured.

He lay back, rolled onto his stomach, and tried to make sense of what had just happened. He knew he ought to get up, to run, to scream, but he didn't know where to run, and he knew that no one would hear him no matter how loudly he might shout. He knew nothing about the plains, and still less about Indians. He knew only that he was lucky to be alive. And he wondered whether the same could be said of his wife.

Getting to his knees, he closed his eyes to keep

the world from spinning. Bracing himself with both hands on his thighs, he opened his eyes again. Everything was blurry, and his head felt as if it had been split in two, but he struggled to his feet and walked toward the screen of willows that nearly brushed the ground with their feathery branches. Pushing through, he shielded his eyes from the bright sun and scanned the hill that sloped up and away from the creek. There was no trace of Susan or her captors, which didn't surprise him.

He started back through the willows, floundered across the creek, and came out into the sun again. He was halfway to the road before the reality hit him, and he threw back his head to scream, one long quavering shriek, "Suuuuuuuuusaaaaaaan!" He bent over then and threw up, his gut wrenching as if someone were twisting it with white-hot tongs.

He started to shiver, and his teeth chattered despite the heat. He spat out the sour taste of the puke and stumbled into a run that was almost mindless. He could see the wagon, knew he had to get to it and somehow get it back to town.

The team sensed his approach and pranced skittishly in the traces, raising their heads and nickering as he hauled himself into the seat, where he doubled over once more, this time with the dry heaves. He felt as if he were being turned inside out, his body convulsing as wave after wave of nausea wracked him.

Pulling the reins loose, he snapped them, whistled to the team, and waited. The horses strained, and the wagon began to move in an odd lurch until he remembered to release the brake, when it spurted forward. He turned sharply, the wagon tilting onto two wheels and nearly spilling him from the driver's seat. He had to rein in the horses for a few seconds. His eyes stung with the bright light, and he realized he'd lost his hat. For a moment, he thought about going back to find it.

Without looking, he groped under the seat for his rifle, hauled it up, and set it beside him on the seat. "A day late and a dollar short," he muttered. He felt like a fool for having left it behind, but guns were not second nature to him, even after a full year, and he wondered whether it would have made a difference. Maybe, he thought, it would have. But maybe it would have gotten us both killed.

Reaching for the buggy whip, he cracked it once, then again, trying to get the horses moving. He was too disoriented to think clearly. Looking at the whip handle, he remembered how Susan had teased him the day he brought it home. "You don't need that thing," she'd said. "Unless you bought it to use on me."

He hadn't laughed. Instead, he'd scolded her. He'd been horrified at the notion, and now, remembering it, he shuddered. It seemed that he scolded her often, too often, as if she were some reckless child instead of a grown woman. He was sorry now he hadn't laughed with her more, learned to cherish her spirit instead of trying so hard, and so futilely, to harness it.

Once he reached the road, he pushed the horses harder, listening to the creak of the wagonbed as it twisted and turned, rising and falling as the wheels clattered over bumps in the dirt road. It would take him nearly an hour to get back to the house and another fifteen minutes to reach the town of Chandler. Even then, he'd have to wait. The sheriff would want to send to Fort Lyon for an army detachment and a scout, someone who could follow the trail the Indians had left behind and, more important, someone who knew what to do when and if they were found.

He tried not to think of Susan now, how terrified she must be, if she was even alive. He brushed that thought away, but liked even less what replaced it—the notion of Susan falling victim to some rapacious savage. He'd heard the stories, every gruesome detail. He'd heard what happened to white women when they fell into Indian hands, and a woman as young and beautiful as Susan would be . . . well, that was something he didn't want to think about. Not at all.

Hansen was having trouble breathing. Every inhalation stabbed him in the chest, and he felt lightheaded. The trees shimmered as if they were underwater, and the sun beat down on his bare head, matting his fine hair with sweat until it lay like clumps of waterweed over his brow. His throat was parched with the short, rapid breaths he was taking, and his tongue thickened in his mouth until it felt like a piece of shoe leather.

When his house came into view, he felt a momentary elation, almost as if he had managed to forget what had happened just an hour before. As he neared the lane, he slowed the team, then negotiated the gate, narrowly missing a collision with one post, and urged the team into the yard.

Jumping down from the wagon, he ran to the pump, jerked the handle several times until water started to gush from the spout, then leaned over to relieve his thirst, gulping the water until his stomach felt distended. Ducking his head, he jerked the handle several more times, letting the rush of cool water drown him for a moment, soaking his hair. He straightened up then, feeling the water trickle down under his denim shirt. Hansen ran a hand through his hair, combed it with his fingers, and then went inside for a towel.

When he had dried his hair, he fished a comb from his pocket, restored some semblance of order to his appearance, then went to the bedroom and started peeling off his damp shirt. Tossing the shirt onto the bed, he got a clean one from the dresser. He stood in front of the mirror, the fresh shirt dangling from one hand. He looked so frail, pathetic even, his skin sickly white, his stomach a bit flabby. At twenty-nine, he was already soft, too soft for Colorado, too soft for anything, he thought.

He shrugged into the clean shirt, tucked it in, and adjusted his belt. Bending slightly, he stared at himself in the mirror for the second time that morning, but the earlier uncertainty had been replaced by contempt in the face that stared back at him from its cold eyes.

Taking a deep breath, he turned his back, walked out of the house, not bothering to lock it, and climbed back into the wagon. Still bareheaded, he jerked the reins and turned the team with more impatience than skill, and headed back out to the road. Chandler was just a couple of miles away now, and its proximity seemed to calm him a bit.

Ten minutes later, he could see the roofline of the Chandler Hotel. The tallest building in town, at three stories, its mass seemed to pull him forward like a magnet, and he began to pick up speed. By the time he reached the edge of town, the wagon was almost out of control, the horses running in near panic as he slapped the reins again and again against their backs.

The sheriff's office was all the way at the other side of town, and Hansen careened down the middle of the main street, drawing stares and excited shouts from the few people on the wooden walks in front of the stores. He set the brake too hard and locked the wheels. The wagon skidded to a halt, kicking up a cloud of dust.

Hansen was still half in the wagon when Sheriff Matt Bell appeared in his office doorway.

"Holy smoke, Reverend," he hollered, "what the hell's wrong with you?" Bell hitched up his belt and stepped out onto the boardwalk.

Hansen nearly lost his balance as he tumbled the rest of the way out of the wagon, and Bell had to jump from the boardwalk to steady him.

A small crowd had started to gather now, as people came running from every direction to see what the fuss was all about.

Hansen panted, swallowed hard, then gulped, "Indians—"

"What about 'em?" Bell asked.

Hansen shook his head. "They took my wife. They—"

"Now hold on, Reverend. Slow down a bit."

Hansen nodded his head, aware of the ripple of concern spreading through the crowd. "We were out on Miller's Creek. Susan was ahead of me. I had the hamper, you see, and it was heavy. I stopped to catch my breath and she went down to the creek. I heard her scream and—"

"Indians, you say?" Bell asked.

Again, Hansen nodded. "Three of them. They grabbed her and rode off with her."

"What kind of Indians? Sioux? Cheyenne? Arapaho? What?"

"I don't know. I don't know anything about Indians. I don't know how to tell the difference."

Bell looked at him more closely now, and noticed the ugly bump on Hansen's head. "That's a pretty mean little knot you got there, Reverend. What happened?"

"One of them hit me—"

"You got close enough for an Indian to hit you, and you don't know what he was?" Bell shook his head in disbelief. "Jesus H. Christ!" Then, remembering to whom he was speaking, he said, "Sorry, I just . . . well. And you didn't shoot him?"

Hansen swallowed hard. "I . . . I left my gun in the wagon."

"You left your gun in the wagon. . . ." Bell looked at the small crowd and repeated this intelligence with more than a little wonder. Then, shaking his head, he examined the crowd until he found the man he was looking for. "Pete, you get on over to Fort Lyon and tell Colonel Bledsoe what's happened here. Meantime, I'll ride out to Miller's Creek with the reverend here, and see can we pick up a trail. I'll send somebody back to let you know what we're doin', if we pick one up."

Pete Harley, his deputy, nodded and ran into the office, returning with a Winchester carbine. As he walked toward his horse, the sheriff stopped him. "Pete, you be sure and tell the colonel we got to move quick if we're gonna get Mrs. Hansen back."

Harley climbed into the saddle and galloped off. The sheriff turned back to Hansen. "Reverend, you come along now, show me where this happened." He looked at the crowd again, picked five men, and told them to get their horses. "And bring your rifles," he shouted after them.

He looked at Hansen, not sure whether the minister had any idea what might lay in store for his pretty young wife, and not wanting to be the one to tell him, either. "Somebody lend the reverend a saddle horse. There ain't no time for no wagon." He went into his office and came back out with two rifles and a box of shells, handed one of the rifles to Hansen, booted his own Winchester, then stuffed the shells into his saddlebags, closed the flaps, and laced them.

With one foot in the stirrup, Bell looked at Hansen more intently. "What in hell were you doing out there anyhow? You ought to know better than that."

"A picnic. It was Susan's idea."

Bell nodded. "Next time the little woman gets an idea like that, you talk some sense into her, Reverend. If there is a next time . . ." He swung into the saddle and jerked the reins viciously. This job is tough enough, he thought, without having to save goddamn fools from themselves.

3

Susan ached in every joint. Draped over the back of the Sioux pony, hands and legs bound with rawhide thongs, she was unable to cushion her body from every jolt and bounce as the horse galloped at breakneck speed across the plains. Once they had gotten away from Miller's Creek, the warriors had stopped just long enough to truss her up like a bundle of buffalo skins. Dangling over the pony's bony back, she felt like a piece of meat, a deer carcass, a slab of buffalo.

So far, her captors had paid her scant attention, not abusing her, not even bothering to look at her with more than an occasional glance. Her arms and legs were laced together under the pony's belly, limiting her movement. She'd been working steadily on the bonds that secured her wrists, trying to pull the knots loose with her cramped fingers, but the leather was thick and sturdy, the knot drawn so tight she couldn't get a purchase on it.

She tried then to claw through it, but the thongs were so tight she couldn't nip the leather without tearing at her own skin. Her fingers were numb from poor circulation, and she was forced to give it up. Her head felt as if it were ready to burst. It would be easier to slip into unconsciousness, to try and forget the nightmare, especially when she thought about what lay in store for her once the Sioux stopped for the night. But she was too much of a fighter for that. As much as it hurt, she kept trying to stretch the rawhide, feeling it slice into her flesh like piano wire.

The sun beat down on her back, and the stink of the pony filled her nostrils, mingled with the stench of her own sweat. She was parched and hungry, but the Sioux showed no sign of slowing up. There had been no sign of pursuit, and she kept wondering what had happened to John when the lone warrior had gone back into the willows after him. She had heard that one ear-shattering scream, her name stretched taut as a gumband until it was barely recognizable to her, and that had been the last she had heard. There hadn't been a gunshot, and for that she was grateful, but she didn't know whether her husband was alive or dead. For all she knew, he might be lying there bleeding to death, maybe already dead.

She wanted to think that he had somehow survived, had run for help, and that even now men were somewhere behind her and her captors, looking for her. But she knew the chances were slim, and the longer they went undetected, the harder it would be for anyone to find her.

As it was, the Sioux had the advantages of mobility, knowledge of the terrain, and, once they reached their village, sheer numbers. For a long time, she hung there, her head suspended just inches from the pounding hooves of the pony, her hair tangled in weeds and brush, yanked out by strands and clumps until her scalp began to bleed. Exposed skin was ripped by sharp twigs and thorns, and one shoe was already long gone, the other ready to follow it at any moment.

But she couldn't give up. Not yet. It wasn't fair to John, and it wasn't in her makeup. She was too much of a fighter to throw in the towel before it was absolutely unavoidable. She still had her courage, but it was ebbing slowly, and she fought against the insidious slide into resignation. As long she kept her will to resist, she had a chance, no matter what might happen to her body. She kept telling herself that if she refused to yield, the Sioux could not break her. They might kill her, but that was different, less to be feared, in a way.

It was late afternoon before the ponies stopped, and then the warriors just sat there, looking into a broad valley that stretched away for miles. The warriors were discussing something among themselves, not even looking back to make sure she was still there. Twisting her head, she tried to see what had captured their attention, and the thought crossed her mind that maybe it was a cavalry detachment, maybe a wagon train. But she was unable to see much beyond a few yards of tall grass that surrounded her on the hilltop. And the ponies began to move again almost at once.

When her own mount broke over the crest of the hill, she could see further toward either end of the valley. A narrow band of silver, tinged orange by the late afternoon sun, stretched like a strand of beaten gold in either direction. Far to the north, several columns of smoke twisted like snakes in the wind, but she couldn't see where they came from. Probably a village, she thought.

And she steeled herself, knowing that whatever the Sioux had in mind for her was not that far off. It was impossible to avoid thinking about it, and she wished she had a weapon—a knife, a hatpin, something, anything to raise the cost of her defeat. She knew she couldn't prevent it, but she could exact a toll, maybe even earn enough respect to ameliorate her treatment. It wouldn't be much, but it might make the difference between living and dying.

As the ponies swept down the hillside, she saw the tops of several tipis, the smoke she had seen earlier rising from their smoke holes. It was a small cluster, not even large enough to be called a village, really, maybe a dozen tipis in all, although she couldn't be sure.

As they drew near, women and children on foot ran out to meet the warriors. Soon, she was surrounded by two dozen people, chattering in a tongue she did not understand. She felt hands tugging at the tattered hem of her dress, others poking her. One more venturesome pair slid along her legs, squeezing her calves, her thighs—not sexual, but insistent, the hands of a horse trader examining a prospective purchase.

The ponies stopped now, and the crowd around her head parted, several small hands still tugging at her hair before they fell away. Then she saw the buckskin leggings of one of the warriors. He knelt down, produced a long-bladed knife, and severed the rawhide binding her hands to her feet. The knife disappeared, and arms encircled her waist. She was lifted bodily from the pony's bare back, feeling very much like a sack of grain as she was dropped over the warrior's shoulder. The women chuckled as the warrior moved away from the ponies, reaching out with his free hand to tousle the heads of a few of the smaller children as he waded through the tiny throng.

She twisted her head this way and that, trying to find a friendly face, but there were none to be seen. The children looked only curious, as if she was some rare specimen none of them had ever seen before, and the women looked, if anything, dispassionate, as if they would have preferred she not be there but didn't feel strongly enough about their objections to make them public.

A tipi loomed up then, its buffalo-hide sides decorated with a dozen intricate drawings, the colors brilliant in the late-afternoon sun. The warrior ducked, crawled through the door-flap with her still draped over his shoulder, then stood again. The tipi was open on one side, where the hide covering had been rolled up to let in the breeze, and she could see a dozen pairs of tiny knees where the children lined up along the open wall then dropped down in unison, as if the move had been rehearsed a hundred times.

She saw an older woman sitting by the fire pit,

working beads on a leather pouch. She grunted, set the pouch aside, then said something to the warrior before she got to her feet. She moved stiffly, as if her old bones were unwilling to cooperate.

He set her down before answering, then walked to the flap and loosened the ties holding the hide in a roll. He yanked the wall down, and suddenly there was nothing but the orange light of the small fire for Susan to see by.

The warrior pulled his knife again, knelt by Susan's curled form, and jerked her hands roughly. He inserted the tip of the blade between her wrists and sliced through the rawhide. The sudden release made her wrists hurt, and she had to tear the severed thongs away where her flesh had folded over them. Deep, raw, red welts encircled both wrists, and she rubbed them briskly, trying to restore circulation to her numbed fingers. Her hands felt as if they were full of quills, and the tingling nearly drove her mad. The warrior turned his attention to her feet, cut the thongs binding them, then stood. He said something that made the old woman laugh, but Susan could only look from one to the other, her face blank with incomprehension.

The warrior left then, without ceremony or, as far as Susan could tell, a word of good-bye to the old woman. Susan rubbed her ankles, kicked off her one remaining shoe that had defied gravity and the odds by clinging to her foot, and tried to stand, but her limbs wouldn't work the way she expected.

The old woman moved close to her, one hand darting like an angry blue jay as it picked burrs and seed hulls from Susan's matted hair. The old woman was more efficient than tender in her ministrations, and several times Susan felt her head jerk as a particularly persistent burr refused to let go.

When her hair had been made relatively free of vegetation, Susan ran a hand through it, trying to undo the tangles, but knots kept catching, and her scalp was sore where small clumps of hair had been torn loose, so she stopped.

She looked down at her dress then, its hem dirty, full of pollen smears and fine brown dust, rent in several places so that it looked more like a collection of rag strips than a garment. The old woman moved to one wall of the tipi and came back with a small basket. Motioning for Susan to sit down, she sank to her knees and patted the buffalo robe beside her, waving for Susan to come closer.

She said something that sounded as if it were meant to be soothing, and smiled, her wrinkled face crinkling still more around her dark eyes. Reaching into the basket, she removed an ornate bone comb and held it out for Susan to take. Hesitantly, the young woman reached out for the comb, leaned toward it to admire the handiwork, and realized it had been manufactured in Philadelphia. "Whiteman comb," the old woman said with a quiet chuckle. Then, as if to make certain she had been understood, she repeated the phrase, this time louder: "Whiteman comb."

Susan started to work on the knots and tangles, and the old woman watched her curiously, as if she had never seen a comb used in quite that way before. It was slow going, and eventually the old woman sat down to resume her beadwork.

As she worked at her hair, Susan watched the old woman, saw how the stiff fingers fumbled with the tiny beads. It was obvious that she had the skill, but the dexterity she had once possessed deserted her. The old woman mumbled to herself whenever she would lose her grip and a bead would spurt from her fingers like a grape jetting from its skin. The bright color would arc like a shooting star across the fire pit, catching light from the flames until it skittered off into the darkness on the other side.

The old woman must have sensed that she was being watched, and she smiled, almost apologetically, as if to say, *I used to be able to do this with no problem.* The smile was tinged with sadness, and Susan wanted to tell her it was all right, that age was cruel to everyone, but she didn't know how, and was afraid to try, for fear her comment would be taken as criticism.

Susan knew enough about pride, had seen how her grandmother had struggled as her body betrayed her. She saw the once flexible fingers, that had flown across the keys to render Beethoven and Chopin flawlessly, beginning to stiffen and stumble. It had pained her then, and it pained her now, and for one brief moment, there was no difference between the two old women, one long dead, now just a memory, and one there before her, an aching body struggling to retain its dignity.

Before she realized it, she had begun to cry. And for a long time, as her body wracked with sobs, she thought she would never stop.

4

Sheriff Bell led the small scouting party out of town at a gallop. Before the town line was passed, John Hansen was already falling behind. Bell glanced over his shoulder, saw the minister having difficulty, and sent the handful of men on ahead. He slowed his mount to let Hansen catch up.

"Reverend, I know you're not much of a horseman, but you got to try and keep up, at least until you show us where it happened."

"I'm trying, Mr. Bell, but—"

"You got to try harder, dammit. A pretty woman like Mrs. Hansen in Sioux hands and all, well, I don't like to think about what could happen to her. She'll be lucky if it hasn't happened already."

Hansen nodded his head, but his heart wasn't in it. The prospect of bouncing his rear end off a saddle for the next hour was too unpleasant. He flapped his knees against the sides of the borrowed horse, but the big chestnut didn't seem to notice. Bell shook his head impatiently, then spurred his own mount on ahead.

Hansen tried his best, but the gap between him and the rest of the men slowly widened, until he was almost a quarter-mile behind. Hansen saw one man peel off, turn his horse and sit, hands draped over the saddle horn, waiting, while Bell pushed on. Hansen, by the time he reached the waiting man, was dispirited, and the rest of the small band was more than half a mile ahead.

As he caught up to the waiting man, Hansen recognized him as Burton Fletcher, a cowhand from one of the large ranches outside Chandler. Fletcher had the reputation for drinking too much and working too little. He liked to pick fights with unwary cowboys. He wasn't much of a fighter himself, but he never seemed more alive than when picking himself up off the floor of a saloon, brushing the sawdust from his jeans, and buying drinks for the house.

"Reverend," Fletcher said, "I reckon you and me will be riding drag on this here drive. Sheriff Bell's pretty anxious to catch up to them Sioux before they get too far. Said he'd meet us at the bridge over Miller's Creek, unless he picks up the trail, in which case he'll leave somebody at the bridge to tell us what's what."

Hansen smiled stiffly. "I appreciate your staying behind, Mr. Fletcher, but there's no need. I assure you I'll get there eventually."

"No trouble. I ain't exactly anxious to pick a fight with some Sioux bucks. They're hell on wheels, especially when they got a chance to have a little fun with a white woman." Fletcher offered a smile that suggested he could just imagine what sort of fun it might be. Then, as if realizing he was talking to the woman's husband, he added, "No offense, Reverend. But you know how it is with Indians."

Hansen licked his lips. "Yes," he said. "I know how it is with Indians." Nothing Fletcher might have been thinking could compare to the horrors rattling around inside his own skull. He looked up at the sky, at the sun now high overhead, and took off his hat to wipe his brow.

"Better kick that damn horse," Fletcher said. "We ought to get moving."

Hansen clucked to the chestnut, smacked his knees against its ribs, and felt a little jolt as the horse picked up its pace. Fletcher fell in beside him.

"You ain't been west too long, have you, Reverend?"

Hansen shook his head. "Just about a year is all."

"Whatever made you come? Don't seem to me like you're all that comfortable out here."

"I'm a minister of the church, Mr. Fletcher. Comfort is not high on my list of concerns."

"Pretty woman like Mrs. Hansen, I reckon she wouldn't mind a little comfort though, would she?"

"Susan understands the demands of my work. She's as committed to it as I am."

"Whatever you say, Reverend."

Hansen was irritated by the undercurrent of Fletcher's words. It seemed to him almost as if the cowboy took some perverse pleasure in Susan's predicament. He clamped his jaws shut, and kicked the horse hard enough to get it moving at a trot.

"Whoa, hang on there, cowboy," Fletcher shouted. "You're gonna leave me in the dust."

Hansen heard the thud of hooves then as Fletcher's mount moved up behind him, then alongside. The cowboy started to say something, but Hansen cut him off. "Look, Mr. Fletcher, if you don't mind, I really don't feel much like talking right now."

"I understand. Worried about the little woman. Can't say as I blame you. Them Sioux bucks can be pretty hard on—"

"Shut up, for God's sake, will you? Just shut up!"

Fletcher chuckled, and moved out ahead. Hansen hung on grimly as the chestnut bounced him unmercifully. It seemed as if he was always going the wrong way, slamming his body into the saddle until his spine felt like jelly. But he wouldn't give Fletcher the satisfaction of his slowing down.

He was breathing hard with the effort of hanging onto the reins and trying to stay in the saddle. Sweat already soaked the clean shirt, and by the time he saw the glittering band of Miller's Creek, he was nearly ready to cry. But that would have been all Fletcher needed, so Hansen bit his lip and promised himself he'd make it down into the valley. He could dismount at the bridge, maybe even rest for a bit.

When they reached the bottom of the valley and the road bent north along the creek, Hansen could see several men standing under the trees just across the bridge. Fletcher yelled and waved his hat. One of the men waved back, and Fletcher turned in the saddle. "Reckon they didn't find the trail, Reverend," he shouted.

Hansen didn't answer, not wanting to draw any conclusions because he was afraid to face the few that occurred to him. He clucked to the chestnut, squeezing the animal between his legs to hold himself still, and endured the last tooth-jarring quarter of a mile in silence.

Bell walked out of the trees to meet them as they rode up. He did not look happy.

"You find anything, Sheriff?" Fletcher asked.

Bell shook his head. "Not a damn thing. There's a few tracks on the other side of the creek, but they peter out pretty quick. Nothing I could follow. We'll have to wait until the army gets here."

"Maybe it wasn't Indians, anyhow, Sheriff," Fletcher said, swinging out of the saddle. He gave Bell a broad wink. "Maybe that pretty little gal just plain run off. Maybe livin' with a preacher was too dull for a high-spirited little filly like Mrs. Hansen. What do you think?"

Bell frowned. "I think you best watch your mouth, Burt. No call to be talkin' like that. It was your wife, you'd be pretty sore somebody cracked a joke like that."

"It was my wife, she wouldn't be bored. I can tell you that much." Fletcher giggled like a schoolboy, and flashed a yellow-toothed grin at Hansen.

"Burt," Bell snapped, "button it up. I ain't gonna tell you again, now."

"Just funnin', Sheriff."

"You save your funnin' for something funny."
Bell turned to Hansen, who was still in the saddle. "You might as well climb down, Reverend.
It'll be a couple hours before the army boys get
here. There ain't nothing we can do till they
do."

Hansen nodded. He had delayed dismounting,
because he doubted he had the courage to
remount once he did. But a couple of hours might
be respite enough even for *his* aching bones. He
slid from the saddle and nearly lost his balance.
Bell reached out to grab him by the shoulder, and
the minister winced as the Sheriff's powerful grip
clawed at his collarbone.

"You think the army will be able to find her,
Sheriff?" he asked, once he was on the ground.

Bell nodded. "Sure do. They'll send one of their
scouts, most likely. Some of them boys can track a
flea through the desert, if they have to. The thing
is, we don't have no idea what we're lookin' at.
You said there was three of 'em took Mrs. Hansen
off, but they could be part of a big war party. I
know Colonel Bledsoe pretty well, and I know
what he'll do."

"What's that?"

"He'll send a squad, maybe six, eight men, plus
the tracker. There's no doubt it's a bunch of
Sioux, but no way of telling how many. He'll want
to know what he's up against before he sends a
column out. Maybe we'll get lucky. Maybe it was
just a small raiding party, and we'll find them
before they hook up with their main band. In that
case, we can handle it right off. But if there's a big
party of Sioux out there somewhere, then we're

gonna have to wait for reinforcements. That'll take a day, maybe more. The army don't do nothing in a day they can spend a week on."

"But Susan . . . what will—?"

"You best not worry your head about that now, Reverend. Maybe nothing'll happen. Sometimes a few young hotheads do something like this and the old men set them straight right off. Nobody gets hurt. Most likely that's what's happened here."

"Sometimes it ain't so pretty, though, Reverend," Fletcher said. "And then the woman gets—"

Bell moved so quickly, Fletcher never saw it coming. The next thing he knew, he was sitting on his rump, wiping a trickle of blood off his chin. "I told you to shut up, Burt," he said. "Now maybe you see I meant it."

"No call to go and do that, Sheriff," Fletcher said. His words were garbled a bit by his thickened lip, and it was apparent that his tongue had gotten caught between his teeth when Bell hit him. He had a lisp now, and bloody spit spattered his shirt as he spoke.

"No call to go runnin' your mouth when you don't know what the hell you're talkin' about, neither, Burt. Now you go on over with the other boys or you get your sorry ass out of here, either one. You understand?"

Fletcher nodded.

Bell took Hansen aside. "Don't pay any attention to Fletcher," he said. "He just likes to ride folks a little, see can he get under their skin. He don't have the sense he was born with, and he's got the manners of a dead skunk, but he'll leave you be now. You want, I'll send him on back to Chandler anyhow."

Hansen shook his head. "No, thank you, Sheriff. I appreciate it, but if a man of the cloth can't turn the other cheek, how can he ask others to do it?"

"Out here, Reverend, a man turns the other cheek, he most likely gets a bruise on both of 'em."

"Maybe that's why I'm here, Sheriff."

Bell shook his head. He wasn't exactly thrilled with Fletcher, but he had little more use for what he regarded as the starry-eyed idealism of the minister. Life was hard, as far as he was concerned too hard for the likes of Hansen. And the truth of the matter was that Fletcher was right. If she survived the ordeal, which was by no means certain, the chances were good she would not be the same Susan Hansen who had ridden out that morning for a picnic with her husband.

Bell at least half believed it might be best for the reverend, and for Susan, if they didn't find her at all. But there was no way in hell he was going to say so, even if Hansen should ask, and Bell, who was not a praying man, muttered one now, hoping he didn't.

5

The old woman shook her head, then got laboriously to her feet and walked over to Susan, where she wiped the tears away. By mimicry, she gave Susan to understand that she should resume what she had been doing and stood over Susan while she combed her hair. Several times, she reached out to help. The gnarled hands moved with some difficulty, but they were not unkind as they picked at the tangles.

Outside, Susan could hear the sounds of the small camp, and she wondered how long it would be before someone came for her. Only when she'd addressed the question a third time did she realize it had two answers—sooner or later, the people of Chandler would learn of her kidnapping, even if John . . . even if he hadn't survived. But she knew, too, that one of the warriors, probably the one who had swooped down on her and draped her so unceremoniously over the horse, would also come for her.

The old woman hummed as she worked, her voice rich and strong, the voice of a woman so much younger than her years. She was relaxed, even comfortable at her task, despite its physical frustrations, as if she had done it a thousand times. Susan found herself wondering what the old woman's life had been like, how she had managed to survive for so long with such apparent good humor. But there was no way to communicate with her, even assuming the old woman would be willing to answer her questions.

After a half hour, her hair finally free of seed hulls, burrs, and long, stiff weeds snarled in tangled strands as if they had been braided in, the knots all gone, Susan looked up as the old woman walked around to face her. The old woman scrutinized the younger woman, tilting her head from side to side. When Susan tilted her own head to mimic the old woman's movements, she earned a smile. The old woman said something, then chuckled.

Moving into the shadows of the tipi near the wall, the old woman fumbled with a dark bundle, then moved back toward the fire, shook out a buckskin dress, and held it out to Susan, gesturing that she should stand up. Susan got to her feet, and the old woman signaled for her to turn around. Susan turned her back, then felt the weight of the buckskin against her back as the woman held the dress up for size. She grunted, apparently satisfied, and grasped Susan's shoulder to spin her around, thrusting the dress toward her with another grunt.

Susan reached out for the dress and nodded.

"Thank you," she said, feeling silly, knowing the old woman wouldn't understand her words. The crone grunted again, then stepped briskly toward her, grabbed her by the arm, and tugged her toward the tipi entrance.

As the flap started to move away from the opening, a flurry of tiny feet darted away. The old woman ducked outside, still holding onto Susan's arm, tugging her down and out through the entrance.

The children flooded back now, encircling the two women and chattering among themselves. Some of the more adventurous reached out to tug at Susan's dress and one, a little girl, held Susan's hand and placed her tiny forearm against the larger, paler forearm of the captive. She seemed confused by the difference in complexion and standing on tiptoe, reached out to rub Susan's cheek, as if to see whether the pale color would come off. She looked at the cheek, then at her fingertips, and backed away, shaking her head.

The old woman waved her arms to shoo away the children, then resumed tugging on Susan's arm as if it were a leash and the young woman some wayward puppy. They moved past several of the tipis where women, sitting in groups of three or four, stopped what they were doing to look at the strange duet with unexpressive faces and flat, dark eyes.

Susan felt as if she were on display, a freak in a touring medicine show. They were headed toward a clump of willows, not unlike the one where her ordeal had begun. Walking with evident difficulty, the old woman dragged her through the curtain of branches down to the edge of the wide creek. She started to pull at Susan's buttons, not quite sure how to get them to work, and Susan folded her hands over the gnarled fingers for a moment, patted them and shook her head no.

The old woman bobbed her head energetically, then started to fumble with the buttons again. She stopped for a moment, pointed to the water, and Susan understood what was wanted. Nodding in agreement, she undid the buttons one at a time, slowly, so the old woman could watch. After the third one, the gnarled hands reached out for the fourth, popped it through the buttonhole, and smiled. Satisfied that she had learned the trick, she stepped back and let Susan finish.

The tattered dress fell around her ankles, and she stepped out of it, pulled her chemise up and over her head, and stepped into the water. It was cold, and she felt her skin pebble with the chill. She walked cautiously, not sure how deep the water might be, or what might lie beneath the surface. Cold and clear, the water was deep, and little light made it through the dense layers of willow branches surrounding her.

The creek reached her hips, and she bent to cup her hands, then splashed the cold water over her chest and shoulders before dropping to her knees and letting the water surround her. The old woman muttered something, then vanished through the branches. Susan ducked under, letting the cold current cover her head, and for a moment she thought about trying to drown herself, opening her mouth and sucking her lungs full of water, but she knew she couldn't do it.

Turning on her back, she pushed further out, floating with the current lapping over her, the tiny slaps of the water cresting over her shoulders and breasts like miniature hands. She swam a few strokes, then stopped, feeling the weight of her legs drag her down until her extended toes just reached the bottom. The water was chin-deep now, and she pushed toward the near shore a step or two until she could stand flatfooted.

The old woman reappeared then, her hands full of some dark green plant Susan didn't recognize. Squatting at the water's edge, the old woman waved her closer, took three or four of the thick, rubbery leaves, and mashed them in her palm. A soapy foam formed in the cupped palm, and the old woman rubbed it on her forearm, then offered the rest of the greenery to Susan.

She soaped herself all over quickly, one eye on the willows as if she expected to see someone spying on her. The scent of the crushed leaves swirled around her, and soon she was covered with the fragrant foam. She moved back into the water to rinse it off, and lay back once more to soak. Her bones ached, and every joint felt as if it had been set on fire.

The old woman clucked to her, but Susan ignored the summons. She didn't know what was going to happen next, and this brief moment of serenity had to be treasured. Once more, the old woman clucked, and this time Susan gave in. She paddled toward the shore, climbed out, and felt the trickle of water over her skin. The old woman handed her the buckskin dress and a pair of moccasins.

Standing on the grass at the water's edge, she pulled the heavy dress over her head, tugging it sharply to get it down over her hips. The soft leather kept sticking to her damp skin. She sat down to slide the moccasins on. Even with the heavy dress, she felt naked, vulnerable in a way she could not explain. But she felt less frightened now, as if the water had washed away her initial terror, leaving a vague dread in its place.

The old woman walked toward the overhanging willow branches and ducked through. For a moment, Susan could see one dark hand holding the branches in a bunch; then the old woman let go, and the curtain fell back into place. Susan took one step, then stopped, looking around her, and before she realized it, she was running, not toward the willows, but toward the creek. She hurled herself in and started to swim, and was halfway across before she heard the old woman shouting.

She reached the opposite shore and hauled herself out of the creek, clawing at the roots of some underbrush nearly at the water's edge. On her knees, she turned and saw the old woman disappear through the willows again, shrieking at the top of her voice. Susan got to her feet, weighed down by the heavy dress, which was now waterlogged and hampering her movements. It clung to her thighs like a pair of arms, but she pulled the hem up to mid-thigh and started to run. She stumbled through the brush, not caring how much noise she made.

She could hear more shouts now, the shrill cries of the old woman punctuated by the deeper, more resonant voices of several men. She ran faster, ignoring the branches that whipped at her bare legs and snatched at her hair.

Breaking through the brush, she found herself in a stand of cottonwoods. Beyond the trees, the land sloped uphill, covered in tall grass. She ran parallel to the treeline, her lungs burning, her legs aching. Unused to the soft leather of the moccasins, her feet seemed to find every rock and root in her path, but she ignored the pain and pumped her legs as fast as she could.

It occurred to her that she might not be postponing her fate so much as hastening it, but it didn't matter. She didn't want to be here, and she would rather die than be brought back.

Angling out into the grass now, she started up the slope. The voices behind her continued to shout, but she didn't dare look back for fear of losing her stride. She knew that if she stumbled and fell, she would not have the strength to get up again. The thought of lying there in the grass trembling like a frightened rabbit was more than she could bear.

The voices were coming closer, but still she refused to look back. Let them catch her if they could, she thought. The crest of the hill was no more than a hundred yards ahead now, and she was beginning to think she might make it. She had no idea what lay on the other side, but whatever it was, it had to be better than what lay behind her.

She could hear footsteps now, and the swish of legs through the tall blades. Her pursuers had stopped shouting, saving their wind for the pursuit. The grass began to thin, and she could move more easily now, but her strength was fading. Every breath was like the stab of a knife blade, and her ribs felt as if they would slice through her flesh. She pressed a palm against them, nearly stumbled, and reached out with one hand to keep her balance. The ground started to flatten out, and she began to hope again that she could get away. The footsteps seemed to be fading away, and once more she glanced behind her to see four Sioux standing, watching her. One of the men was smiling. Far behind them, at the bottom of the slope, several women stood in a tight knot, watching as if it was a game.

The ground leveled off, and she took another step before she realized why her pursuers had abandoned the chase. She was on a bluff. The ground sloped gently for a few yards, then fell off in a sheer drop. She skidded to a halt, three or four feet from the edge. She looked over and down. It must have been two hundred feet, a sheer wall of reddish rock. Mounds of boulders and broken slabs that had fallen from the face lay jumbled against the base of the cliff.

And she knew now that they were watching her, waiting to see what she would do, whether she would jump rather than be recaptured.

Turning to face the four Sioux, who had started to walk slowly up the last hundred yards, she bared her teeth and waved a fist at them, daring them to come closer. They were all laughing now, as if it didn't matter to them whether she jumped or not. Maybe, she thought, they are even hoping I will.

On hands and knees now, she leaned out over the edge, looking for some sort of handhold, thinking she would try to climb down the sheer rock face, but there was nothing she could grab onto. The nearest of the warriors was only fifteen yards away now. He was still smiling, but he had one hand in the air, as if to calm her. Except for a bone-handled knife in a sheath at his hip, he was unarmed, but that made no difference. He was too strong for her.

But she was not ready to give up. She stood up again, moved a couple of feet closer to him, then ducked into a crouch, wagging her fingers at him, daring him to come closer. Still smiling, he complied. She recognized him now as the one who had captured her.

He stopped for a moment, said something, his voice surprisingly soft, almost tender, as if he were trying to calm an hysterical child. But Susan would have none of it. She moved sideways, sliding along the edge of the cliff. He charged suddenly, and she feinted one way, then ducked back in the opposite direction, swinging a clenched fist that grazed his cheek. The other warriors laughed, and he turned to glare at them for a moment. Susan took advantage of the diversion to lash out with a foot, catching him in the chest. He fell backward, but grabbed her ankle as he landed.

She struggled free, crab-walking, and he dove at her, catching her just as she lost her balance and started to fall. She could see the blue sky all around her, and was convinced that she was going to smash herself to pieces on the rocks below, but he held on. Her head and shoulders were out over the edge, and she knew that if he lost his grip, she would die.

She lay there, still, and he looked at her, hauling himself up on hands and knees, his fingers like a steel claw around her ankle. He pulled then, dragging her away from the precipice, his eyes filled with fear, not for himself, but, she realized, for her, and for what might have happened.

She felt her head bang against the edge of the rock and, with the earth beneath her again, she closed her eyes. Taking a deep breath, she screamed once. Then, for the first time since her capture, she allowed herself the luxury of terror.

6

John Hansen was brooding. Sitting by himself under a cottonwood, leaning against the peeling trunk and keeping it between himself and the other men, he tried to keep his mind off Susan and her predicament. It was already late afternoon, and there still was no sign of the army. Bell had sent a galloper back to try to find the troops, not even sure they were coming and, if they were, how many there would be.

By four o'clock, the sheriff was pacing, trying to keep his temper from igniting. The rest of the men sat by the creekbank, three of them playing poker for blades of grass. Burton Fletcher kept making jokes at Hansen's expense, and they had long since ceased to amuse the others, but Fletcher seemed oblivious to the stony stares that greeted each labored innuendo at Susan Hansen's expense.

Bell, to keep himself from throttling the cowboy, tried to stop his ears, but every time he turned and saw the smirk on the man's face, he wanted to pull his Colt and shoot the bastard. At four-ten, turning once more toward the road, he spotted a pale haze hanging just above the hilltop, and he breathed a sigh of relief. It had to be the army, and he sprinted to his horse.

With one foot in the stirrups, he hollered for the others to wait where they were, then swung up into the saddle and headed toward the road. As soon as he reached the rutted track, he spurred his mount and galloped up the hill, lashing the roan with the loose ends of his reins.

When he reached the hilltop, he pulled up, stood in the stirrups and shielded his eyes against the late-afternoon sun. It was the army, sure enough, but it was a pitiful handful. By a quick count, he came up with ten men, and at least one of those was probably Pete Harley, the man he'd sent to look for them. But he thanked God for small favors, and nudged the roan into a walk, heading down the far side of the hill toward the advancing patrol.

At the bottom of the hill, he reined in to wait. He spotted Pete Harley, riding beside a young officer, probably a second lieutenant, and Harley waved, then said something to the young officer. A moment later, Harley kicked his horse and spurted forward. The officer followed him, while the rest of the men continued at their steady trot.

"Sheriff," Harley said, nodding toward the officer, "this here's Lieutenant Randolph Harrison."

Harrison pulled off his leather gloves, tucked them under his thigh, and reached out a hand.

"Sheriff Bell, pleased to meet you. Colonel Bledsoe sends his regards."

"How is Tim?" Bell asked.

Harrison smiled. "Ornery as ever, I guess, Sheriff. At least, he's been that way since I was posted to Fort Lyon. He's so good at it, I figure it must be a lifelong habit."

Bell laughed. "It is that, Lieutenant."

"What happened here, Sheriff?" Harrison asked, suddenly serious.

"A handful of Sioux bucks jumped a local preacher and his wife. They knocked him over the head and near killed him. Run off with the woman. I lost their trail pretty quick, top of the hill on the other side of the creek. I hope you got a tracker with you."

"I do. One of the best, Scotty Horgan."

Bell glanced toward the cavalry patrol, now just a hundred yards or so up the road. "I know Scotty," he said. "You're right. He's one of the best, if not the best."

"Any idea what prompted the attack?"

"None. The reverend was kind of shook up, and I didn't see any point in leaning on him till you got here. I figure he can tell it once better'n he can tell it twice."

Harrison nodded uncertainly. "I suppose."

Bell wheeled his mount around. "I guess we might as well get going. Be nice to close the gap before sundown, if Scotty can figure out which way to go."

He started back up the hill, and Harrison moved up alongside him. "How many men you got with you, Sheriff?" he asked.

"Six, counting Pete, here, and not counting the reverend, who ain't much good for a thing like this. Fact is, I think it'd be best if we sent him on home."

"Will he go?"

Bell shrugged. "He should, but I don't know whether he will or not. We can always order him to, I guess. He's like a fish out for water out here. And if we get into a scrape with them Sioux, I don't want to have to worry about some greenhorn preacher getting in the way."

Harrison didn't answer, and when they reached the top of the hill, Bell pointed to the slumping figure of Hansen leaning against the cottonwood. "That's him," he said, "under that tree yonder."

Harrison nodded. "Maybe it would be best if I talked to him alone to start. No sense getting him upset, if we can avoid it."

"You be my guest. Try to make him get the point quicker than he's used to. Kind of long-winded."

Harrison waited for the patrol, ordered a ruddy-faced sergeant to take the rest of the men down to the creek and water the horses, then brought Bell with him as he rode over to where Hansen was sitting, his head slumped forward as if he was sleeping. When the two men dismounted, Bell realized that Hansen was weeping. His shoulders barely shook, and the sound was more of a mewling whimper than anything else.

Harrison walked over to stand beside him, but Hansen didn't look up. Bell squatted in front of him. "Reverend, Lieutenant Harrison here wants to talk to you if you feel up to it. About what happened and such."

Hansen nodded his head, once, the movement barely noticeable. He looked up then, and Bell saw that the minister had rubbed his cheeks raw. His eyes were red-rimmed and swollen, and dirty lines squiggled down both cheeks. As if sensing where Bell's attention was fixed, he sniffed, then rubbed his cheeks with the cuff of his right sleeve, spitting on it to moisten the dusty cotton.

Bell walked away while Hansen and the lieutenant spoke. He saw Scotty Horgan walk across the creek, and followed him. The scout was dressed in denim pants and an army shirt, although he was a civilian. Tall and muscular, Horgan was almost a legend on the plains. His skin had the look of new leather. His pale hair and mustache, almost but not quite white, made him look older than he was. He'd spent nearly twenty of his forty years leading wagon trains along the Oregon Trail, leading cavalry units through the ocean of grass and the trackless forests of the northwestern plains, and swearing at one pig-headed West Pointer after another who came west thinking to lick the Indians single-handed.

Horgan knew as much as any white man about the Sioux, and knew personally a dozen of their chiefs and three times as many of their prominent warriors. He had hunted buffalo with Red Cloud and deer with Man Afraid. He had cussed at Crook and thumbed his nose at Sheridan. More than a few Sioux considered him a friend, and he was as good a friend to them as a white man could be, which was not always quite as good as he wanted to be. But he also knew enough about Sioux customs to know that Susan Hansen could be in more trouble than anybody, including her husband, dared think about. Finding her was not the problem. He could do that. Getting her back unharmed was something else again, and he wasn't at all sure that anyone could do that. It would depend on who had taken her and why.

Bell followed the tall scout up the grassy slope on the far side of Miller's Creek. Horgan knew he was there, but didn't acknowledge him. Instead, he kept his head bent, moving slowly, stopping every few yards. Now and then, he looked up the hill as if trying to see what might be on the other side. When he reached the top, after what seemed to Bell to be an eternity, Horgan finally turned to him.

"That little man know what a mess he's got his woman into, Matt?"

Bell shrugged. "Search me, Scotty. I don't think so. If he did, he never would have come out here in the first place, I think."

"How'd he happen not to get himself killed?"

"That's the question, I guess. Said he left his gun in the wagon when they walked to the creek. I found the picnic hamper they brought, so I guess they're as dumb as he made them sound."

"Just could be they won't hurt the woman, then. They were looking for trouble, they would have lifted his hair. Things have been pretty quiet for a few months. There's always a few troublemakers, some with cause, some not. Looks to me like there was five horses, one empty."

"He said there's three bucks. At least that's what he saw."

"Probably out hunting, then. Had horses for the game, and didn't find anything worth taking, until they spotted Mrs. Hansen."

"Can you find her?"

"Sure I can."

"Can we get her back?"

"Maybe. But the sooner we move, the better for her."

"You know where they went?"

Horgan pointed off across the valley. "Looks to me like they headed northwest. Probably a small camp somewhere fifteen, maybe twenty miles. Any more than that, they would have moved the camp. This was probably the outer limit for them. It'll be after sundown before we get there, but that might be a good thing. We can see how many of them there are."

"What's Harrison like, Scotty?"

"Better than most, I think, but I don't really know. Bledsoe likes him. Says he's not likely to go off half-cocked like the young ones so often do. Must teach that back east. Most of them get themselves killed before they unlearn it out here. And Tim's been wrong before."

"You want me to bring your horse?"

Horgan shook his head. "No, I'll walk back, talk to the reverend before we leave. A few minutes one way or the other won't make much of a difference. If she's still alive, and I think she probably is, then we have time. If she ain't, then it don't make much difference."

"Why'd they take her, Scotty?"

Horgan looked thoughtful. Bell wasn't sure whether he was sifting through possible options or reluctant to answer him at all. He waited patiently while Horgan leaned over, pulled a long, slender weed, and peeled its dark green skin away to the soft white inside. It seemed to Bell almost as if Horgan were looking for the answer in the weed. He ran the weed across his tongue, then tossed it away. "Tastes like licorice," he said.

"You going to answer me or not, Scotty?"

"Good-looking woman, from what Pete says. That's one reason."

"Are there others?"

"Sure. Sioux are like anybody else. They got lots of reasons. Some of them make sense and some of them don't. And not just to white men. Sometimes they want somebody to help out with the chores. It could be that simple. Sometimes they have an old person, usually a woman, who can't tend to herself. If she doesn't have any relatives in the village, they get her one, adoption, sort of. Maybe that's what happened here. It'd be best for Mrs. Hansen if it is."

"And if not?"

"If not, we'll find her out there somewhere with her throat cut and her legs rubbed raw."

7

Horgan rode point. He was seventy-five or a hundred yards ahead of the small column, his eyes glued to the ground. Matt Bell stayed behind, trying to keep Hansen's spirits up. The minister had resisted Harrison's suggestion to return home, and the sheriff had agreed to let him accompany the soldiers so long as he kept up.

Every so often, Horgan would dismount and examine something on the ground that none of the others could see. Harrison, who was just a year out of West Point, was still amazed by the scout's ability to follow tracks that, as far as he was concerned, didn't exist.

"If I didn't know better," Harrison said, "I'd swear the man had an overactive imagination. I don't see a damn thing and he's telling me when they stopped, how long they rested, and who said what to whom."

"Scotty's about as good as it gets," Bell told

him. "I spent three years at Fort Laramie, in the cavalry. Scotty was there then, and he already had a reputation. I remember once a bunch of Sioux hit a wagon train, killed three or four people, and lit out. Scotty found them in two days. It was like he knew where they were going even before they did. Used to have a Sioux wife, but she died of cholera some years back."

"He married an Indian?" Harrison was amazed. "I never thought that—"

"Look, Lieutenant, the Sioux have their ways and we have ours. But they're people, just like we are. Some of 'em are good people, and some of 'em would slit your throat as soon as look at you. But if I had my choice of enemies, I'd pick the Sioux over the white man every time. At least they fight by the rules."

"Their rules," Harrison said. "Don't forget that, Sheriff."

"Their rules, true enough, but rules all the same. A Sioux calls you his friend, he don't stick a knife in you when your back is turned. Can't say that about a lot of white men."

"You aren't one of them Indian lovers, are you Sheriff?" Harrison asked.

"Nope. What I am is a lawman. It's my job to see that folks leave each other alone, red and white. That don't always happen, but I don't judge a man by the color of his skin. It's what he does that matters to me. I have seen my share of atrocities, but they weren't all committed by Indians. You'd do well to think about that, before you get your ass in a sling. Out here, that can happen in the wink of an eye."

"You don't have to tell me how to handle Indians, Mr. Bell. I know my job as well as you know yours."

"That so?"

"It is. We find these red devils, and I'll show you what I mean."

"We find these red devils, as you call 'em, and you let Scotty do the talkin'. You stick your nose in before you know what's what, you'll likely get it cut off. And it won't help Mrs. Hansen none, neither."

Hansen, who had been silent for a long time, spoke up. "Maybe you'd better let the army do what it does best, Sheriff," he said.

Bell looked at the minister, and it was obvious he wanted to give him an earful, but he bit his tongue. "Let's find them first, Reverend," he said. "Let's just find them, before we worry about anything else, all right?"

"Easy to say. It's not your wife they took."

Bell was losing his patience. "Look," he snapped, "if you knew so damn much about it, you wouldn't have left your gun in the goddamn wagon, now, would you? So don't you go telling me you're an Indian expert all of a sudden. You don't know jack shit about the Sioux, or we wouldn't be here in the first place."

"The lieutenant knows his job." Hansen leaned forward a bit to look at Harrison. "Isn't that right, Mr. Harrison?"

The lieutenant nodded. "Damn right I do."

"I still say we let Scotty decide."

"Mr. Horgan works for me, Sheriff," Harrison said. "I give the orders, and he follows them.

That's the way it's always been, and I don't see any reason to change things now."

"You find your hair bunched in a Sioux fist, a scalping knife pressed against your forehead, maybe you'll think different, Mr. Harrison." Bell spurred his mount ahead, leaving the patrol behind. He caught up to Horgan, who was just climbing back into the saddle.

Horgan looked at him with a quizzical expression. "Something wrong, Matt?"

Bell shrugged. "I don't know. I think your Lieutenant Harrison is a horse's ass, and he's got him another one in the Reverend Hansen. We let those two have their way, we'll have us another Sioux uprising on our hands."

Horgan grinned. "Harrison's not the worst I've seen. But they're all the same, really. They always come out here full of piss and vinegar. Guess they pour it into them back east. But they learn. If they live long enough."

"I don't give a damn how long they live, just so long as they don't get me killed right alongside 'em. I figure to spend a few years sittin' in a rocker on my front porch before I pack it in."

"Front porch?" Horgan laughed. "Hell, Matt, you don't even have a house yet, do you?"

Bell laughed, too. "I'm workin' on it."

"You figure to christen it with a bottle of champagne, like they do with ships?"

Bell snorted. "Hell, Scotty, on what they pay me, I'd better figure on a bottle of vinegar." Horgan nudged his horse forward. The sheriff rode alongside him. Behind him, Bell could hear the jingle of sabers and spurs. It was not a comforting sound.

It was getting near sundown. The wispy clouds caught fire as the sun sank toward the horizon, exploding into tongues of deep orange flame. The green hills darkened, and the valleys filled with shadows. Bell kept glancing back over his shoulder at the patrol, and every time he looked, Hansen and Harrison were deep in conversation. For a moment, he wondered whether the minister was trying to convert the lieutenant, or vice versa; then he decided he didn't really want to know. Better to let the fools keep one another company.

"What do you figure we got here, Scotty?" he asked, when they had ridden for nearly a quarter-hour in silence.

The scout shrugged. "Probably just a small hunting party. Most likely eight, ten tipis. The buffalo are getting scarce in these parts, and the Sioux have been breaking up into small bands every year, after the sun dance."

"That doesn't sound good."

"Why not, Matt?" Horgan turned to look at him, a puzzled look on his face. "A small group, we have a chance to get the woman back without a fight."

"I don't figure that would please the great Indian fighter back there. I think he'd just as soon try to avenge Fetterman all on his own. Make a name for himself, get himself in the newspapers back east."

"Not likely. We handle it right, we just talk to the Sioux and tell them there won't be any punishment, and they'll hand her over."

"If she's still alive."

"She's alive, all right. We'd have found her body by now, if they were going to kill her."

"You sure about that?"

Horgan winked. "You ever known me to be wrong about something like that?"

"No. But times are changing, Scotty. You know that as well as I do. There's an ugliness now. The rules have changed, and it's the innocent folks who are getting caught in the middle."

"Nobody's innocent, Matt. You know that. Put yourself in a pair of moccasins for a minute." He swept one arm in a broad arc. "All this used to be Sioux land. Before that, I reckon it belonged to some other tribe. But it's been Sioux for a hundred years, at least. Every day when the sun comes up, your land is a little smaller. There's less food, more wagons, more white faces. How do you think you'd feel?"

"Same as the Sioux do."

"Damn right. Now, you think you'd make distinctions, one white face from another? Or would you say, like some of the firebrands do, you got to draw a line somewhere, make a stand. I sure as hell know what I'd do."

"But women and children? They fair game, Scotty?"

"I been in enough villages where the corpses were so thick you couldn't take a step without bumping into one. Most of them were women and children, Matt. You're right, the rules are changing, but the Sioux didn't change them, we did."

"We getting close, do you think?"

Horgan nodded. "Couple miles, maybe three. Fact is, I think it'd be best if I went on ahead. You think you can hold young Mr. Harrison here till I get back?"

"Give it my best shot." He reined in, then turned his horse to wait for the lagging patrol.

Harrison spurred his mount forward. Hansen did his best to follow along, but Harrison left him in the dust. When the lieutenant reached the two men, he jerked the reins hard. "What's going on?" he asked.

Horgan answered. "We're getting close. I'm going on ahead, see if I can pinpoint the location."

"They'll get away," Harrison argued.

"No, they won't. If they break camp and move on, it'll be in the morning, just after sun-up. And they *will* move on. But we're asking for trouble we go riding up after dark. They won't bother to see what we have in mind before they start shooting."

"And just what is it we have in mind, Mr. Horgan?" Harrison demanded.

"See can we convince them to let Mrs. Hansen go. If she's there."

"You don't think they'll tell us, do you?" Harrison made no attempt to conceal his contempt for such misplaced trust.

"Of course they will. Most likely there's a subchief in charge of the camp. More than likely, he's itching for a chance to turn the woman loose. We handle it right, we give him the excuse he needs."

Harrison nodded. "I don't like it, but I guess you know best."

"I do," Horgan said. "Make no mistake about that. I do."

8

Susan expected to be punished for her escape attempt, but the warriors had been gentle, treating her with deference and, it seemed to her, a kind of respect. It seemed almost as if they were in awe of her for trying to make a break for freedom. They had held on to her all the way back across the creek and into the old woman's tipi, but she had not been beaten or even handled roughly. Once she was inside, the old woman had shrieked at her, venting a spleen so passionate that even the warriors cowered, and, as soon as the old woman's back was turned, they slunk away, one pausing at the entrance to hold a finger to his lips and shake his head, as if warning Susan not to argue with the old woman.

But Susan didn't need to be warned. She knew she had pushed her luck about as far as it would go. The next time, she knew, would not be so tame.

When she was finished her diatribe, the old woman sat down on the buffalo robes by the fire, her arms crossed, black eyes catching the flaring firelight and glaring at Susan across the fire pit. Her expression was stern, seemed to demand an explanation that both women knew could not possibly be given, not with the unbridgeable gap of language yawning between them.

But the anger faded quickly. Near sundown, the old woman had pulled Susan outside and with much waving of hands and exasperated shakes of the head given her to understand that she was to eat. Strips of buffalo meat were sizzling on a cook fire, and the old woman snared two, one for each of them, then handed Susan her portion before tearing into the other. The meat was hot, the grease burning the roof of her mouth, but she was famished, and she managed to get it all down without too much difficulty. It tasted better than she had expected, reminding her of beef—a little gamier, a little stringier, but pleasant all the same. She tried to tell herself that it was just because she was hungry, but she knew better. Until today, it had been hard to think of these people as anything but savages, but everything she had seen since her capture flew in the face of that notion.

After they had eaten, the old woman tugged her back inside and forced her to sit by the fire. Sitting next to her, Susan watched as she continued with her beadwork, fixing one after another of the shiny, colorful beads to the front of a buckskin dress. The ancient fingers seemed to work almost mechanically, as if they would have go on even in the old woman's sleep. But the beads kept darting away, and the machine was in need of repair.

When she had finished, the old woman looked up, tilted her head, then poked herself in the chest with a finger. Susan watched, not certain what was expected of her. Then the finger touched one of the beads in her lap, before returning to the old woman's chest. She leaned toward Susan then, her face expectant.

Susan said nothing, and the old woman touched the bead again. Tentatively, Susan, said, "Bead?"

The old woman shook her head. Touching the bead again, she then touched two others, shaking her head negatively each time. Once more, and once more expectant, the old woman touched the blue bead. Susan tried again. "Blue? Is that it? Is it the color?"

Once more, the old woman shook her head no.

The door flap rustled, but Susan was so intent on the old woman's antics, she didn't turn to see who had entered. Again the ancient finger touched the blue bead, and again, Susan said, "Bead? Bead?"

"She tries to tell her name," a voice said. "Blue Buffalo Woman is her name."

Susan snapped her head around to find herself staring into the face of the man who had kidnapped her that morning. "English . . ." she said. "You speak English!"

"Little bit," the warrior said. "I have been to Fort Laramie many times, when we were living on handouts from the Great Father. That was long ago, before we learned he was not great and was not our father, only the white man's father."

The old woman watched the conversation with rapt attention, as if trying to understand the alien words by sheer force of will.

"What did you do to my husband? Is he—"

"We did not harm him. Hit in the head, but—"

"Why did you take me here?" Susan demanded.

"Blue Buffalo Woman is old. She cannot take care of herself as she once did. She has no family."

"But you can't just drag me away from *my* family!"

The warrior shrugged. "It is our way. It is the old way. A good way, I think. I have seen your old people. They have no teeth and their arms and legs no longer work. If they have no family, they die by themselves, with no one to look after them, no one to send them to *Wakan Tanka*. It is the same with us. But sometimes—"

"Wakan Tanka?"

"Your preaching men say 'the great spirit.'"

"God? You talk about God to me, and you have kidnapped me."

"I don't know the word."

"Captured me, made me a prisoner."

"There are many whites, and not many Lakota. Blue Buffalo Woman needs you. The whites do not need you."

"But I—"

"They do not need you. Blue Buffalo Woman needs you."

Susan, suddenly a schoolmarm confronted by an obstinate pupil, shook her head in exasperation. "What is your name?" she demanded.

"In your language it is Red Hawk."

"Red Hawk, do you have a family?"

He nodded. "Yes."

"A wife . . . a woman?"

Again, he shook his head affirmatively.

"Would you be sad if she was taken from you? Taken away, so that you didn't know if you would ever see her again?"

"Yes."

"How do you think my husband must feel? Don't you think he feels the same way you would feel if someone took your wife away from you?"

"I would not let someone take my wife away." He said it so simply. For Red Hawk, she knew, it was not a statement of conviction, just a fact.

Susan argued, knowing that there was no room in his world for a contradiction to that simple fact. But she had to try. "Still, it could happen."

"Never."

"They will not let you keep me here against my will. You must know that."

Red Hawk shrugged. "We will see. Tomorrow we move the camp."

"But the soldiers, they will find you. And they will punish you."

"They will not find us. And they cannot punish us. Punishment is from the white man's law, but his law is for the white man, not the Lakota."

"I will run away again."

"And I will bring you back again. Blue Buffalo Woman needs you."

"You can't keep me here. I will keep on trying to run away until I escape for good."

Blue Buffalo Woman had been following the conversation, her head swiveling back and forth, always fixing her dark eyes on the face of the speaker, trying to glean from their expressions what she could not from their words.

Now, she muttered something, and Susan looked at Red Hawk. "What did she say?"

Red Hawk laughed. "She says we talk much, and while we talk you learn nothing."

Susan had to smile. "See, I am worthless to her. Tell her that. Tell her that I cannot do things for her because I do not know what to do and I won't know how to do it, even if I am told."

"She will teach you."

"I don't want to learn. Tell her." Angry again, Susan snapped, "Tell her that! Tell her exactly what I said. Word for word."

She watched while Red Hawk translated, keeping her eyes fixed on Blue Buffalo Woman's face. When the warrior finished speaking, the old woman looked as if she had been slapped. Her face seemed to crumble, the stern mask breaking into pieces, leaving behind another mask of indescribable sadness. She muttered something, her voice breaking, then turned away.

"What did she say?" Susan demanded.

Red Hawk chewed on his lip, but did not answer.

Once more, Susan barked, "What did she say, damn you!"

Red Hawk turned as if to walk away. Susan, amazed at her temerity, approached him, reached out to touch his shoulder, and let her hand rest there, but he swept it away with an angry swipe of his hand.

Again, Susan asked, this time softly, "What did she say, Red Hawk?"

He turned then, nodded almost imperceptibly, as if to confirm his decision to tell her. "She says she is old, and that it is time to die. She said you are right, that we cannot make you stay if you don't want to stay."

Susan felt the air rush from her lungs. "I see."

"Tomorrow, when we move our camp, you will stay here. I will give you food for a few days."

"Thank you." Then, almost as an afterthought, she asked, "What will happen to Blue Buffalo Woman?"

"That is nothing for you to care about." He made as if to leave, but Susan stopped him with a sharp command.

"Wait. I want to know. What will happen to her?"

"She will stay, too. She does not want to go with us."

"But—"

"It is what she wants."

"But she will die. I mean, with no one to help her, she'll . . ."

"Yes. She will die."

"But that's barbarous. You can't leave her here like that."

"We are not leaving her. She is choosing to stay and we cannot make her come if she does not want to come."

"But yet you were willing to take me from my family, make me come someplace I did not want to be."

"That is not the same thing. You are the enemy."

"Why am I your enemy? You don't even know me."

"You are white. That is all I need to know. The white man does not care that one red man is not another. And he has taught us not to care that one white man is not another. These are the white man's rules, and we are starting to learn them, how to live by them."

Susan looked at Blue Buffalo Woman for a long time without speaking. The old woman seemed to sense that somehow she was the subject of the conversation, but she looked confused, and not a little frightened.

"So," Susan said, "tomorrow, you will pack your things and ride away, leaving this woman here to fend for herself."

"Yes."

"You can't."

"I can and I will. There is little food, and every day there is less. The buffalo are gone, and . . ." He stopped for a moment, his voice catching, and he turned away before continuing. "I do not want to do this thing. I did another thing, and you told me that it was wrong. Now you tell me that this, too is wrong. If you know the right thing, please tell me what it is."

And he was gone.

9

Scotty Horgan was happy to leave the idiots behind. He had a short fuse in the best of times, and every time he found himself leading a pack of quarrelsome brats out into the wilderness, he swore it would be the last time. The army seemed to choose two kinds of men, and only two—swaggering buffoons who were too full of themselves to have any room left over for common sense, and whiskey swilling morons who were too full of booze to make use of what little sense they had.

Harrison was itching to show everyone how tough he was, and while it was true that the young lieutenant was not the worst of his kind, it was also true that the best was not half good enough. The army never seemed to get it through its collective head that Indians were every bit as courageous and half again as resourceful as it was. For the most part, the brass thought with their muzzles, as if firepower compensated for any intellectual shortcomings of their commanders.

Horgan could point to a dozen examples of just how foolhardy the army approach was, but a dozen more would not have weighed one whit more in the balance. Now, riding through the twilight, he hoped he was not going to strike a spark that would explode once more into bloody war. He had no doubt he would find Susan Hansen. He had considerable doubt whether she would be in any shape to appreciate it. There was just no telling. What happened to the woman would depend on who took her and why. But he would learn the answer to those questions soon enough. It was what came next that troubled him.

Getting the Hansen woman back from a small hunting party would be feasible, but might tempt Harrison into some sort of stunt they would all regret. Getting her back from large war party would be impossible without a full column, but Horgan wasn't sure the lieutenant would know the difference.

After an hour's ride, he reined in. The moon was just beginning to peek over the horizon, and he dismounted to wait for it to clear the treeline ahead of him. Its light would help him and hamper him. He could see better, of course, but so could anyone else, and a Sioux party of any size, with a newly taken white woman captive, would be nothing if not alert. He wanted to wait a few minutes, let his eyes adjust to the moonlight, before pushing ahead. He had to be close, close enough that he might hear a pony nicker, maybe an argument between husband and wife. Maybe the mournful flute of some heartsick suitor would come wafting toward him on the breeze. And maybe he would find nothing at all.

As at home as they were on the plains, the Sioux were like anybody else. That was the one thing the army didn't seem able to get through the armor plated skulls of the officer corps. Monthly changes in policy from Washington did nothing to help, either. But it was Horgan's ability to put the color of skin aside and put himself in the other man's shoes that had made him so successful. It was also what had spawned his increasingly less concealed admiration for the Sioux and their ways.

The way the Sioux lived made sense to him now, a kind of sense he had been too young and too bullheaded to recognize when he'd first come west. But he'd learned a thing or two since then, more than a little from the young wife whom he still missed, even after ten years. He just hoped he knew enough to fend off the calamity he felt bearing down on him like an avalanche.

When the moon was fully risen, its full disc a baleful white eye gliding above the treetops, he turned to look at his shadow on the ground. It was sharp enough that he would have to worry about it. Tugging his horse into a stand of pines, he hobbled it, took his Winchester rifle, and stuck some extra shells into his pocket. Reaching into his saddlebags again, he pulled out a package of rolled leather. Sitting on the ground, he pulled off his boots, then pulled on knee-high moccasins, Apache style, with the curled toe, and pulled them all the way up over his jeans. It would be warm, but boots were out of the question now. One snapped twig could get his throat cut or draw an arrow or bullet that he would never hear until it was too late.

Reconnaissance, the army called it. There were times when he thought of it as more like nosy neighbors prying into other folks' business, but this wasn't one of those times. Getting to his feet, he stamped each foot once to make sure they were fully seated in the moccasins, and started forward without a backward glance at the horse, which was snuffling among the trees, its hooves tamping the matted pine needles nervously.

He climbed the hill ahead of him, saw the creek far below, catching moonlight on its ripples, in some places so bright it looked like sunlight boiling up from somewhere underground. The slope ahead was steep, studded with brush in the tall grass, but he wanted to get away from the trees to lengthen his sight line. If there was a Sioux camp nearby, and he had no doubt there was, there would be smoke. He might see it in the moonlight even before its tang alerted him.

He sprinted down the slope, his speed as much to keep his balance as because he was in a hurry. Halfway down, he slipped on the dewy blades, caught himself with one hand, and regained his stride for the rest of the trip. Here and there, clumps of trees hugged the water's edge, but he could see quite a distance in either direction along the broad creek. It looked too deep to wade across, and he resolved to follow the near bank.

The Sioux, like most Indians, camped on the water. They depended on it for so many things—

sanitation, drinking, cooking—and there were usually large herds of horses, three or four for every person in camp, sometimes even more. He had seen herds of six or seven thousand head grazing near some of the larger villages. The animals alone, with their incessant thirst, would have tethered the bands to a watercourse.

So far, there was no sign of smoke, and he sniffed deeply every twenty or thirty feet. Even a dead fire, no longer smoking, would have left traces in the air. He'd gone nearly a mile before he smelled the smoke. Two steps later, he found a few horse apples, fresh, no more than a couple of hours old, more proof that he was getting close. Bending near the water's edge, he saw the prints of several unshod ponies. That spurred him on, and he moved more quickly now.

Glancing at the sky, he could just make out wispy traces of smoke, like translucent feathers drifting toward the hill on the opposite bank of the creek. The fire had gone out, and these were its last gasps. He stopped to listen. The silence was broken only the squeak of a bat overhead and, somewhere in the distance, the snarl of a catamount. The camp was probably small. Generally, larger villages had their share of night owls, people who, for whatever reason, couldn't or didn't want to sleep and seemed not to care whether anyone else slept either.

If it was a hunting party, there would probably not be any dogs, which would enable him to get fairly close, but whether he could get close enough to learn if Susan Hansen was being held prisoner, and if so, where, was another matter.

Short of seeing her with his own eyes, evidence would likely be circumstantial, at best. But he was in no position to be choosy.

Two hundred yards later, he saw the first tipis, their crossed sticks jutting up through their tops like dark fingers clawing at the sky. He counted nine, but couldn't be sure whether he'd seen them all. Seventy or eighty horses drowsed on a grassy slope behind the tipis. Somewhere on the hill above them, he knew, a picket would be watching, probably a young boy. Horgan wanted to get close, but there were limits on just how close he dared go. It would do no one any good if he were to alert the Sioux. They would probably bolt, and even if they didn't, there would be no way to get close enough tomorrow to negotiate for the woman's release. And if they caught him, the best he could hope for was two prisoners, the worst would be two dead whites.

Not knowing who the leader of the small band might be was a handicap. If the man in authority was someone he knew, then a simple conversation might put a quick end to the situation. But if the leader was a young hothead looking to make a name for himself, then no amount of peaceful persuasion would secure Susan Hansen's release. But he wasn't about to walk into the camp now and ask to speak to the chief.

There wasn't much time, because Harrison was antsy to begin with, and Horgan knew that if he stayed away too long, the lieutenant might just get it into his head to come looking for him, and for a little trouble. Backing up a bit, he moved parallel to the creek, but far enough away that the trees behind him gave him their cover. The moon was off to his left, floating high above the trees now, and he wanted to remain as inconspicuous as possible until he reached the other end of the small camp. He had the creek as a buffer, but if he was spotted, it would not stop pursuit. Horseless, he would be forced to stand and fight, because there was no way on earth he could outrun the Sioux ponies. Hiding wouldn't work, either, because, once alerted to his presence, they would not rest until they ran him down.

As he moved slowly past the tipis, he counted, and this time came up with eleven. Two of them had been hidden by a clump of cottonwoods on his first count. The change was not significant, but he wanted his report to Harrison to be accurate. He sat still for a long time, staring at the hillside behind the camp. The tipis, backlit by the moon, were reflected in the surface of the creek. So far, he had seen no sign of a picket on the hillside. The horses milled in small clumps, sometimes bobbing their heads, sometimes nickering. Once or twice, one of the stallions bolted, the sudden solitary thunder of his hooves echoing across the water. But it was just nerves.

He still didn't know whether Susan Hansen was in the camp, and he didn't have a clue how he could find out. He kept toying with the notion of moving closer, maybe even crossing the creek and trying to slip in close enough to hear some stray talk, maybe learning enough to decide whether or not the white woman was a prisoner in one of the tipis. He didn't want to take the risk, but unless he got lucky, and soon, he wasn't going to have a choice.

As the moon shifted, something caught his eye downstream. At first, he thought it was something alive, something splashing in the water at the edge of the creek. But when he stared at it, he changed his mind. He wasn't sure what it could be, but it was absolutely silent, and he knew it wasn't alive.

Keeping to the shadows, he moved downstream. He was going to have to cross after all. Not until he was a quarter-mile past the edge of the campsite did he dare approach the water's edge. When he did, he slipped in quickly, making no noise and holding his Colt revolver and the Winchester high overhead to keep them dry as he waded across. He muttered a silent prayer that the water never got deep enough to force him to swim.

He groped carefully with his toes, the water-logged moccasins making his legs heavy and clumsy. But when he passed the midway point, the water came just past his chin and, by standing on tiptoe, he was still able to walk. As the water grew shallower again, he leaned into the current, sending a blunt-nosed **V** across the shimmering surface. He kept his fingers crossed that no one came down to the bank, because the ripples just might be visible from the camp.

When he hauled himself out on the far side of the creek, he holstered the Colt, squeezed some of the water out of his moccasins and pants, then moved back upstream, this time keeping to the edge of the trees. The brush hampered him a little, but he wanted the cover, even with the need to move slowly.

He spotted the thing, whatever it was, when he was still a hundred yards away. It floated in and out of the moonlight, fluttering sluggishly, like a giant broken wing. He still didn't have any idea what it might be, but knew he had to find out. He was trying not to imagine the worst. At fifty yards, he made a guess, and at twenty-five, he changed the guess to a certainty. For a moment, he thought about letting it go at that, but changed his mind. He could see Hansen's pinched features, skeptical, even accusatory, could hear Harrison's hot temper getting the better of him, and he decided to move all the way in.

At the water's edge, he bent over to fish it out of the creek, hauling it carefully, not lifting it to avoid the sound of dripping water, but dragging it across the dirt and grass of the bank. It was a dress. And he knew, without ever having seen it or her, that it had been worn that morning to a picnic by Susan Hansen.

10

The camp lay quiet below them. Horgan lay beside Lieutenant Harrison, who used binoculars to try to pierce through the pre-dawn gray.

Trying once more to convince Harrison to take it easy, Horgan said, "I think maybe we—"

But Harrison waved a hand to shut him up. "Wait a minute," he snapped. "Let me get the lay-out down, dammit!"

Matt Bell watched the two men from a few yards away. He had come to share Horgan's antipathy for the lieutenant, but his hands were tied. Once he'd asked for the army to step in, he had ceded control over the search for Susan Hansen. Now he was wondering whether he would come to regret it. And the evidence that he would was mounting rapidly.

John Hansen, looking forlorn and out of place, paced nervously back and forth. He had seen the dress Horgan had recovered, identified it to a certainty as Susan's, and was now allowing his imagination to run rampant. All manner of indignity and violation butted heads like rutting rams inside his skull, each more barbarous than the other, until he was convinced that Susan had been so brutalized that she would be a drooling idiot, if she survived her ordeal at all.

Horgan had tried to reassure him that the condition of the dress was a consequence of a long, hard ride, and nothing more. There were no bloodstains, he pointed out, and that had to be a good sign. But Hansen refused to believe him. The scout was beginning to believe that some twisted thing inside the minister needed the possible horror to be real, to validate something in him, something neither brain nor soul could explain.

Burton Fletcher was the spark to the tinder, and Matt Bell kept telling him to shut up. But Fletcher had willing ears in Harrison and Hansen, and seemed to take some perverse pleasure in describing the likely abuse Susan had endured. Bell was beginning to wonder whether Susan might not consider herself lucky for having been taken by the Sioux rather than by the besotted cowboy. It seemed that Fletcher was able to give voice to whatever Hansen secretly feared and, in voicing it, made it real not just for the minister, but for the lieutenant as well. The three men had become an unholy trinity. Each man had his own reasons, no doubt, but each of them seemed to need to believe the worst.

Finally lowering the glasses, Harrison clapped Horgan on the shoulder and backed away from the hilltop. When they were below the crest, he stood up, waited for Horgan to do the same, and made a ceremony of replacing his field glasses in their case. Horgan noticed the pale gleam of the gold "USA" on the flawless leather and speculated the letters might stand for Unusually Stupid Ass, but he knew better than to voice the suspicion aloud.

"Doesn't look to me like they'll be much trouble, Mr. Horgan. We have plenty of firepower, enough to take care of a handful of redskins, anyhow."

"Like I said, Lieutenant, there doesn't have to be any trouble at all. You let me and Matt ride down there and talk to whoever the headman is, and we can settle this thing pretty quick."

"They'll cut you to ribbons, Horgan. Two men would have to be crazy to ride down there, white flag or no. I just can't allow it."

"What have you got to lose, Lieutenant?" Bell asked. "Scotty knows what he's talking about."

"A good officer does not take casualties when he doesn't have to. His first responsibility is to his command, to keep them safe."

"You pick a fight, you'll get somebody killed, sure as I'm standing here. That doesn't sound like good officering to me," Horgan argued.

"You seem to forget that you are a civilian, Mr. Horgan. I know my business, so why don't you let me do it? You do your part, and there will be nothing to worry about."

"And what exactly is my part, Lieutenant?"

"You got us here, that was half of it. Get us home when this is over. That's the other part. Right now, all you have to do is follow orders."

Horgan was losing his patience altogether. "What are you going to do, ride down there and set the camp on fire, see who runs out of what tipi?" He glanced at Hansen, hoping to sway him. "Or will you wait and pick through the ashes looking for bodies, see which one was Mrs. Hansen?"

"That won't be necessary."

"You don't even know which lodge they're keeping her in. Until you know that, you can't do anything anyhow. Once bullets start flying, you could get her killed by accident. Is that what you want to happen? If it is, I want to see how you write that up for Tim Bledsoe."

"You're out of line, Mr. Horgan." Harrison started to ball his fists, and Horgan noticed it. Part of him wanted the idiot to take a swing at him. Decking the stubborn bastard would be the closest he'd come to pleasure in quite a while.

But Harrison thought better of it, forced his hands to unclench, and took a deep breath. "What are we supposed to do, sit here and wait until hell freezes over?"

"We're supposed to get Mrs. Hansen back safe and sound," Matt Bell said. "That's the first and, as far as I'm concerned, only thing we have to do."

"And I suppose you think we should let these savages go unpunished? So they can do it again, is that it? You want every woman in the territory lying awake at night, waiting for a pack of wild Indians to carry her off to do God knows what to her? Because I don't want that. And I'll do anything I have to do to make sure that doesn't happen."

Horgan stepped in front of Bell to answer. "First off, nobody broke into Mrs. Hansen's home." He looked at Hansen, who seemed to shrink away from the scout's obvious contempt for him. And when Horgan jabbed a finger in his direction, Hansen cringed. "If that damn fool right there had a brain in his head, we wouldn't be here now. You let fools roam around the country unattended, and there's nothing but trouble will come of it."

"You justifying what happened, Mr. Horgan?" Harrison demanded. "Because that's what it sounds like to me."

"No, I'm not justifying it. I'm explaining it. As far as I'm concerned, they were fools who were looking for trouble, asking for it, and they found it. I don't think Mrs. Hansen ought to suffer for her foolishness, but I don't think we ought to risk her life to save it, either."

"Maybe Mrs. Hansen *was* looking for it," Fletcher suggested. "Maybe the reverend there isn't up to giving her what she needs."

The troopers exploded in laughter, but Bell whirled around. He took a step, then another, watching Fletcher back up one step at a time. "Now hold on, Sheriff," Fletcher said. "It was just a joke. I didn't mean no harm."

Bell pointed at him, took another step, and jabbed the finger into Fletcher's chest so hard that it thumped. "I been telling you for two days to shut the hell up, Burt. I ain't telling you no more. You open that ugly yap of yours again, and I swear to God, I'll shut it for you."

Fletcher backed away from the finger. He

started to relax, but Bell wasn't finished. "Now, you apologize to Reverend Hansen."

Relieved that he was getting off so easily, Fletcher mumbled something barely audible. "Louder," Bell demanded.

"I said I didn't mean nothing by it. I'm sorry."

Fletcher could barely bring his eyes to Hansen's belt buckle, but the minister was too embarrassed to care. He just wanted the subject changed, and mumbled, "No offense taken."

Horgan took Bell and Harrison each by the arm and dragged them further back from the hilltop, glaring over his shoulder at the citizens and soldiers to make sure they didn't try to follow. When they were far enough away from the others, he said, "Look, we have got to decide what to do, and we have got to decide it quick. It'll be sunup soon, and once folks start moving around down there, it'll tie our hands. Now, I already told you what I think we should do." He looked at Bell, and asked, "Matt, what do you think?"

Bell shrugged. "I'm willing to ride down there and see if we can't settle this mess peaceable. No point in starting a war nobody wants."

"I don't agree nobody wants a war," Harrison said. "If you don't want a war, you don't go around abducting people. The Sioux started it, and I mean to teach them a lesson they badly need and won't soon forget."

Horgan started to object. "But—"

Harrison, though, waved him off. "Here's what we're going to do. I agree that we ought to know where the Hansen woman is before we make a move, so I think we ought to watch the camp until we get some sense of where she is. Then we'll move in and snatch her. If they don't want to fight, fine. I won't chase them."

"If they don't fight? Man, are you crazy? Those are their homes you're talking about," Horgan exploded. "You charge in there with guns, what the hell do you think they'll do?"

Harrison shook his head. "I can't help that."

"Why don't you send a galloper back to Fort Lyon? Ask Colonel Bledsoe what to do?"

Harrison got furious. "You telling me I don't know how to make my own decisions? You want me to run to Colonel Bledsoe like some schoolboy with a math problem? I'm commanding this unit."

"And doing a damn lousy job of it, if you ask me," Horgan volunteered.

"Besides, if we wait, they'll move on. I'm not interested in chasing these damned Indians halfway across the territory to get back one stupid woman. We're going to move down there now and get as close as we can before sunup. As soon as we have enough information, we'll do what we came here to do."

Harrison stalked off and explained what he wanted to Sergeant Anderson, who relayed it to the enlisted men. Harrison then gathered the rest of the men around him and gave them detailed instructions. They were to leave their horses behind, tethered, with one man to guard them. They were to move in silence and they were not to fire unless they heard the order. "And don't spook their goddamned horses, or they'll know we're here," he added.

In five minutes they were on the move, snaking

down the hillside from two different points, one toward each end of the clearing where the camp sat quietly. Horgan, knowing it was a mistake, went along because he didn't know what to do to stop it.

He slipped off by himself to find the picket. It took him ten minutes. The boy was sitting against a tree, his head sunk in his lap. He might have been asleep, but Horgan couldn't be sure. Working his way around to a point directly behind the tree, he moved forward on tiptoe, knelt at the base of the cottonwood, and snaked an arm around the tree, clapping a hand over the sentry's mouth and pinching his nose.

The boy struggled, reaching for a knife at his waist, but Horgan pinned the arm until the boy stopped struggling. Dragging him into the trees, he cut strips of buckskin from the picket's breech-cloth to tie his hands and feet, then stuffed a handkerchief in his mouth to keep him quiet. After making sure the boy could still breathe, he sprinted after the others.

So far, the camp was still quiet. But Horgan had a feeling it wouldn't stay that way for long.

11

Scotty Horgan slipped in behind Harrison, patting him on the back to let him know he was there. The young officer was startled, and nearly screeched with surprise. "Jesus Christ! Don't do that. I could have killed you."

Horgan smiled inwardly. Not on the best day of your life, mister, he thought. But he said nothing, not wanting to challenge the man. Harrison already seemed to believe that he had something to prove, and Horgan was loath to give him yet another reason. "Sorry, Lieutenant," he whispered. "See anything yet?"

Harrison shook his head. "Not yet. I thought I heard voices a few minutes ago, but I can't be sure. Too far away to hear clearly, even if I knew the language."

Horgan nodded. "How long are you prepared to wait before you attack?"

"An hour or so. No more than that."

"Then what?"

"Then we hit them hard and fast. They'll be too disorganized to resist."

"You ever see the Sioux fight, Lieutenant?"

Harrison shook his head. "No, why?"

"I didn't think so. You would never have said that, if you had."

"You make them sound like they're superhuman, Mr. Horgan. No bunch of savages can match the discipline of a trained army. And our advantage in firepower will overwhelm them before they can regroup."

"Discipline is beside the point, Lieutenant. The plains Indians are used to a different kind of combat. They strike like rattlers and are gone before you know what hit you. Discipline slows you down. Your men will be waiting for orders. If something happens to you, they'll be like headless chickens. The Sioux are used to thinking for themselves in combat. They don't need orders, so they can stay one jump ahead of you every step of the way."

"You forget one thing, Horgan. They have their families down there. They will be hampered by that."

Horgan snorted. "You think this will be the first time a camp has been attacked? You think they don't know about Sand Creek and what happened to the Cheyenne there? You think they don't know how to hold off an attacking force until the women and children are clear, you better think again. The fact is, they'll be even more determined to fight, for that very reason. I still wish you'd reconsider."

Harrison shook his head. "No."

Neither man had anything else to say, and Horgan lay there stewing, trying to decide what he could do to prevent what now seemed inevitable. For a moment, he considered firing his weapon, send the Sioux spilling out of their lodges. But it might not help and it almost certainly would get him arrested. Matt Bell would back him, but the damage would already have been done. And Harrison was almost certain then to take his anger out on the Sioux. As Horgan saw it, they were already in enough trouble.

The sun was due any minute. Already the stars were gone, and the gray cast of the sky had begun to brighten. Horgan surveyed the hillside. The deployment of the men was haphazard, but he couldn't fault Harrison for that. In the darkness, it was more important to get close and find cover than it was to replicate some textbook exercise. Still, the tipis were nearly two hundred yards away, and the ragged line was unbalanced at one end. Only one or two men were past the far edge of the Sioux camp.

Horgan decided to give it one more try. Once the first Sioux appeared, things would start to move, and there would be no time for reconsideration. He crawled over to where Harrison lay behind a clump of brush. "It's still not too late to try my way," he whispered.

The lieutenant shook his head. "We try your way, we give up the advantage of surprise."

Horgan was disappointed but not surprised. He was about to crawl back to his position when movement caught his eye on the flat land below.

He lay still for a moment, then slid closer to Harrison to get out of the line of sight for anyone in the camp. Reaching out with one hand to pull a branch aside, he saw a woman walk toward the water's edge, a clay bowl in her hands. She squatted by the edge of the creek, dipped the bowl half-full of water, then straightened. She started to walk back toward the her lodge, then stopped. She seemed to be staring straight toward Horgan. For a moment her eyes seemed to stare right into his. He was certain he had been seen, and he pressed his chin into the ground.

But a moment later the woman ducked back into her lodge, and the camp was quiet again. Very soon, Horgan knew, the other women would begin to emerge from their lodges and children would be darting in and out among the them.

The first warrior to make an appearance was a tall man, taller than average for a Sioux. He was young and well muscled, his hair braided into a pair of thick ropes falling over his shoulders. He had emerged from the same lodge where the women had come and gone. He stood looking at the sky, looking as if he were searching it for some sort of sign. Almost instinctively, Horgan, too, looked at the sky. If the warrior saw anything, it was of no significance. He crossed the camp and stood at the entrance to the last lodge on the far end.

He started to duck toward the flap then seemed to hesitate. He straightened again, glanced up the hill, and Horgan saw his face for the first time. "Red Hawk!" he whispered.

"What did you say?" Harrison hissed.

Horgan shook his head and held a finger to his lips. When he was sure Harrison would pay attention to the injunction, he silently shaped the word "later" with his lips, and turned back toward the warrior just in time to see him duck through the flap and disappear into the lodge.

For Horgan, it was a mixed blessing. He knew Red Hawk, not well, but well enough to think he could talk sense to him. A nephew of Spotted Tail, the young Sioux was highly regarded by many of the younger warriors. He had a reputation for courage in battle nearly the equal of Crazy Horse's, although he did not have the same influence. If Horgan could convince Red Hawk to surrender the woman without a fight, none of the other warriors would raise a hand to stop it. And, secure in his reputation, Red Hawk would not feel compelled to offer resistance merely for the sake of saving face. That was the good news.

The bad news was also rooted in Red Hawk's character. If he could not be persuaded to surrender Susan Hansen, then there would be a fight, and it would be a bloody one. There was little more than fifty minutes left until Harrison's arbitrary deadline expired. That it was unknown to the people in the small village below as it ticked inexorably away seemed grossly unfair to Scotty Horgan, but he was powerless to do anything about it. Or was he? He found himself praying that Susan Hansen did not emerge from a lodge until he had figured out what to do next.

*   *   *

Red Hawk nodded to Susan, then walked over to squat in front of Blue Buffalo Woman. "Grandmother," he said, using his native tongue, "we will be leaving soon. There will be food for you. Enough for a week. Longer if you are careful."

"That will be enough," she answered.

"I still wish you would change your mind."

The old woman shook her head. "No. I have been a burden for too long. I don't wish to be a burden any longer. I have had my years. The children need to have theirs."

"Both can have their years. I will hunt for you. It is no trouble."

But Blue Buffalo Woman was adamant. "You don't lie very well, Red Hawk. I know how difficult it is. You have your own family. There are other old ones who need your help. You can't feed everyone. You are like Crazy Horse—stubborn. Your mind is like a rock when you make a decision. But a rock breaks if the strain is too great. You will break, too. Already, I can see how you are growing old beyond your years. One man cannot carry all the people on his back, even you with your broad shoulders."

"What is she saying?" Susan asked.

Red Hawk glared at her. "It is of no concern to you. It is Lakota business." He turned back to Blue Buffalo Woman.

"Don't be so hard on the white woman, Red Hawk. She means no harm."

He shook his head. "One need not mean harm to bring it. You know that as well as I do. We would not be having this discussion otherwise."

Susan tried again. "What are you talking about, damn you?"

Red Hawk bit his tongue. He looked at the old woman for a moment, and when she asked what Susan had said, he told her. "You can answer her. It makes no difference to me."

The young warrior nodded. "All right. I will tell her. I will tell her exactly what we are talking about." Turning to look at Susan, he shifted his weight to rest on his knees. "I am trying to make her change her mind. There is no need for her to do this thing. But she says that she will do it."

"Do what, exactly?"

"Stay here."

"Don't try to hide behind words that don't mean anything. Tell me exactly."

Red Hawk sighed. "She will stay here. We will leave food. When the food runs out, as I told you, she will die. That is what she says she wants."

"But why?'

"It is our way. Sometimes, when the weight of an old one is too great, when there is no one to hunt for food, the people leave them behind. Sometimes the old one decides for herself."

"But you can't leave her!"

"The Lakota are free people. I cannot make her do what she does not want to do."

"You have to."

"Why, because it is the white man's way?"

Susan shook her head. "No. I don't know that we are any better to our old people. Probably not. But . . ."

Red Hawk shrugged his shoulders.

"She can come to live with me and my husband.

We will care for her." The words astonished her for a second, but before their echo had faded, she realized not only that she meant them, but that they were natural and right.

Red Hawk smiled sadly. "Maybe Blue Buffalo Woman is right."

"She's *not* right."

"I meant about you. She said that not all whites were bad. She said that you meant well. Perhaps you do."

"Will you ask her? To come with me? I will take good care of her. I promise you."

"No," he said, "I won't ask her."

"Yes," Susan said, balling her fists and taking a step toward him, "you will."

"She will not accept your offer."

Susan moved closer still. Her hands were clenched in front of her, her arms trembling with the strain. Red Hawk thought for a moment that she actually meant to attack him. "You say the Lakota are free people. That means you can't make a decision for her. Not one like that. She has to make it. Ask her, dammit!"

Red Hawk bowed his head for a moment. When he looked up, his eyes were wet. "Go outside," he said. "Go outside, and I will ask her."

12

Horgan saw the woman emerge from the lodge, and he knew immediately that she was Susan Hansen. Harrison didn't react right away, as if he hadn't noticed her. Maybe, Horgan thought, crossing his fingers, it's the dress. Maybe he thinks she's an Indian.

He held his breath, hoping against hope that the woman would go back inside. But Harrison grew tense. He jerked his field glasses from beneath his body and trained them on the front of the lodge. "Damn! It's her. It's Mrs. Hansen," he muttered. Turning to Horgan, he added. "I guess we know which lodge she's in. Are you satisfied now, Mr. Horgan? Can we get on with our business?"

Before Horgan could answer, another woman appeared from one of the remaining lodges, then another, and a third. Within ten minutes, the campsite was teeming with men and women.

"What the hell is going on?" Harrison hissed. He looked at Horgan for an explanation.

"They're getting ready to break camp now. They'll be taking the lodges down and packing everything for the move."

"They're not going anywhere. Not if I can help it."

Harrison started to get to his feet.

"Wait!" Horgan said, raising his voice. But Harrison was not to be deterred. He jumped to his feet and moved out from behind the brush, pulling his pistol at the same time. He raised the gun in the air, then took a step forward. Horgan reached out to grab him and haul him down, but Harrison was too far away. Scrambling to his feet, Horgan moved toward the lieutenant, but he was too late.

Harrison fired a shot into the air and shouted, "Let's get 'em, boys." He started down the hill. The others leaped from cover, and a sharp volley of rifle fire rattled in a ragged line across the hillside.

Horgan saw the Sioux freeze for a moment after the first shot, but the volley thawed them. Every head turned to look up the slope. Susan Hansen ducked back into the lodge. Her husband recognized her, and began to move downhill. As he half ran and half stumbled toward the Sioux lodges, he screamed, "Susan! Susan!"

The warriors ducked back into the lodges and reappeared with their weapons. Several had rifles, and they charged across the grassy clearing toward the bottom of the hill. For fifty yards, there was no cover, and Harrison ordered another volley, but his men were running downhill, and their aims were unsteady. Puffs of gunsmoke mushroomed on the hillside, and Horgan shouted for the men to stop shooting. If they heard him, they chose to ignore him.

Racing down the hill after Harrison, he grabbed the lieutenant. "Stop this!" he shouted. "Stop it now! No one's been hurt yet. It's not too late."

But Harrison jerked his arm free with a snarl. "The hell it isn't."

The Sioux had reached the bottom of the hill now, where there was brush and scrub oak. But the women and children were scurrying into the trees, and Harrison directed his attention toward the fugitives. "Stop them," he shouted. He aimed his pistol toward the fleeing figures and squeezed the trigger. Horgan saw a woman clutch at her hip, saw the bright smear of blood when her hand came away. She screamed and went down on one knee, and a child turned and ran to her. Trying to help the woman up, the little boy lost his balance and fell to the ground beside her.

The rifles were turned now on the fleeing women and children, who darted among the trees, zigzagging from trunk to trunk. The troopers were firing as fast as they could work the levers of their carbines. Hunks of bark chipped from the trees, leaving white scars the size of a human hand. The bullets spanged and whined into the woods as if disappointed to have found wood and bark instead of flesh and bone. Desperate now, Horgan looked for Matt Bell on the hillside, but couldn't find him.

Determined to stop the attack, Horgan charged

down the hill, his hands raised over his head to show the Sioux he did not intend to shoot. "Red Hawk, where are you?" he shouted.

There was no answer. A bullet sailed over his shoulder, and it took him a second to realize it had been fired from behind him. He started to turn then, and another bullet caught him in the thigh. The leg went numb, then collapsed beneath him. He landed heavily on his back. Stunned, he lay there for a few moments, trying to collect his senses, then started to crawl, but the pain was so intense he was forced to stop. He lay there alternately whimpering and calling for Harrison to halt the assault.

Two of the troopers decided to break cover and charged down the hill. Two shots cracked almost simultaneously from the foot of the hill, and both troopers went down. One began to crawl back uphill, moaning, both hands clawing at the grass beneath him. The other lay still, and Horgan knew that no one could stop it now.

The crawling soldier reached a scrub oak and tried to drag himself to his feet by holding onto the trunk. But the small tree couldn't take his weight, and he lost his balance, toppling over, the bent tree arcing over him like a collapsed umbrella. Before he hit the ground, two more bullets found him, and Horgan saw the splatter of blood and the whirling white razors of bone slivers where a section of rib had been blown out by a Sioux bullet.

Two more men charged down the hill, and Horgan realized with a shock that one of them was John Hansen. The minister's face was a contorted mask of hatred as he rushed toward Horgan, and the scout reached out to grab him around the ankles. The minister fell heavily to the ground, losing his white-knuckled grip on his rifle.

Hansen screamed like a banshee, then whirled on Horgan. "You damned idiot. What are you trying to do?"

"I'm trying to save your life, and Mrs. Hansen's into the bargain," Horgan said, unclenching his teeth just long enough to get the words out.

Hansen snorted, his teeth bared like fangs. The tiny teeth caught the red light of morning and winked like rubies for a second before he scrambled free of Horgan's grasp. He got to his feet, his head swiveling wildly as he looked for his weapon. Horgan saw it, but pretended not to.

"You damned fool," Horgan hissed. "You'll get your wife killed."

"The only way to save her is to get her out of here," Hansen said, panting. "And that's just what I intend to do." Once more, he looked around for the gun, spotted it this time, and snatched it from the ground.

Whirling, he plunged on down the hill, leaving Horgan to call after him, "Come back, damn you. Come back before it's too late."

But Hansen ignored him, and Horgan knew with a certainty, as if a giant fist had squeezed the breath from his lungs, that it was already too late. Far too late.

He lay there helpless, tore one sleeve from his shirt, and fashioned a tourniquet with the barrel of his Colt to try to stop the bleeding. He saw

Susan Hansen coming back out of the lodge again, this time struggling as if she were trying to drag a great weight from the tipi. A moment later, Horgan saw why. An old woman followed the white woman out of the lodge, trying to tear loose from Susan's grasp.

Horgan tried to get to his feet, keeping the tourniquet twisted tightly. The leg hurt like the blazes, and he couldn't bend it, but as long as he kept it stiff he thought it would take his weight. A trooper thundered past him, nearly knocking him over, and Horgan called out to him, asking where Harrison was, but the man never acknowledged him.

Two Sioux warriors converged on Susan Hansen, one of them Red Hawk. Horgan saw the young chief try to separate the two women, and when Susan refused to let go, the other warrior took the old woman by her free arm. Together, Susan Hansen and the Sioux brave dragged the old woman toward the trees.

They had almost made it when a bullet slammed into the warrior's body, hitting him high on the back and almost certainly shattering his shoulder blade. Bright blood splattered Susan Hansen's face and arms, and Horgan saw her stare at the mess without seeming to realize what it was. She wiped her free hand on the buckskin dress, then reached up to her face. That was when she screamed.

Even above the sporadic gunfire, the sound seemed unearthly, as if it were coming from somewhere other than the body of the slender woman. It pierced through the sounds of battle, and

Horgan would have sworn that, for a split second, everyone stopped. But he knew it was just an illusion. However, the shriek had drawn the attention of the attackers, and three men sprinted toward the two women and the staggering warrior, who must have sensed their approach, because the warrior let go of the old woman's arm and turned, dropping to one knee and trying to raise his rifle.

One of the white men—it looked like Burton Fletcher—ran straight at the wounded man, sensed that the warrior couldn't get the weapon up in time, and fired point blank, hitting him in the forehead and splattering Susan Hansen with brain matter and blood. Even at that distance, the blood looked unnaturally bright, catching the brilliant red rays of the rising sun. She looked for a moment as if she were bleeding fire.

Susan sank to her knees, losing her grip on the old woman, who stood there trembling, looking first at the fallen warrior, then at Mrs. Hansen, then back again.

Horgan shouted at the top of his lungs, but no one seemed to hear him. Sioux warriors converged on the frozen tableau from several directions. They seemed unwilling to fire their rifles, perhaps for fear of hitting the old woman. Two of them darted forward, getting out ahead of the others, but Fletcher saw them coming, shouted the alarm, and fired his rifle as rapidly as he could work the lever.

Then the two troopers opened up, and one of the charging Sioux stumbled and seemed to cartwheel through the air. His rifle flew out of his hands, its barrel catching the sunlight as it spun away. Horgan continued to hobble down the hill. He saw Red Hawk emerge from the trees, grab the old woman around the waist and lift her to his shoulder, then stagger back into the woods.

The second charging Sioux fell to his knees and fired his rifle once, but the shot sailed harmlessly into the trees, and he fell forward and lay still. Fletcher pointed his rifle at the prostrate form and pulled the trigger, but nothing happened.

Harrison led a charge of half a dozen men, intercepting the rest of the converging warriors. Three men dropped to their knees and the other three stood behind them, and the six rifles worked incessantly, cutting the lead warrior to ribbons and sending the others darting off into the trees.

Red Hawk and another warrior reappeared and reached for Susan Hansen, but Harrison saw him, aimed his pistol, and fired twice. The warrior beside Red Hawk looked at his chest, at the two ugly holes punched just an inch apart, then at Susan Hansen. He reached out with one hand, but his strength deserted him before he touched her.

She knelt beside the wounded Indian, screaming as Red Hawk vanished into the woods, then buried her face in her hands. John Hansen and Burton Fletcher grabbed her, each taking an arm, and dragged her back toward the foot of the hill.

Several of the lodges had been torched, and the air was filled with the stink of burning hides. It was a stench that Horgan had smelled a hundred times, and it never failed to make him sick to his stomach.

His leg gave out on him, and he collapsed to his rump. He loosened the tourniquet and lay back, wondering if he would ever walk again, or live long enough to know. It seemed to grow suddenly dark, and he closed his eyes.

He could hear the sporadic gunfire now fading away. Then it grew completely still.

13

S cotty Horgan's head hurt. Only gradually did he become aware of his surroundings, and it was the noise that first caught his attention, a grinding sound beneath him, as if the earth were gnashing its teeth. He opened his eyes, but the sun hammered them closed. He lay there listening, his lids red and incandescent under the brilliant glare.

His wits were slow to gather. He felt jouncing, something rigid beneath him, and gradually was able to connect the jouncing with the sound of gnashing teeth. He was on a travois. Once more, he tried to open his eyes, this time turning his head until he felt the sun on his cheek, and gradually opened them to narrow slits.

It was starting to come back to him, now. He could remember the battle as fitful bursts of sound came back to him, and sights flashed before his eyes. Burning lodges, women screaming, the stink of gunsmoke all tumbled together like leaves on a rushing current and focused finally as a knot of pain in his leg. He remembered being shot, remembered the tourniquet, and glanced down at his leg as if he could actually see the ball of fire burning its way through his thigh.

He tried to get up, but he was lashed to the travois, across the chest and legs, with only his arms free to move. He waved a hand and raised his head. He heard hoofbeats then, and a familiar voice: "You feeling any better, Scotty?"

Shielding his eyes with the palm of one hand, he opened his eyes all the way. "That you, Matt?" he asked.

Bell grunted. "Figured you'd pull through. You lost a lot of blood, though."

"What happened, did—"

"Just listen," Bell interrupted. "Save your strength. Mrs. Hansen's okay. We lost four men, unfortunately none of 'em men I'd just as leave have seen six feet under. Harrison took a few prisoners—three kids, an old woman, and a wounded buck."

"How many casualties on their side?" Horgan asked.

"Nine that I know of. Two bucks, the rest women and children. A couple of braves rode off, bad hurt, and might not make it."

"This didn't have to happen, Matt."

"You know that and I know that, but right now, I figure we're the only two who do. But," Bell sighed, "it did happen, and there ain't nothing we can do to change that."

"What happens now?"

"Everybody goes back to normal, I guess, gets on with their lives. The same thing that usually happens when some damn fool makes a mess of things."

"I'm going to talk to Colonel Bledsoe. Harrison has to be punished. He can't be allowed to get away with this."

"Ain't likely to be punished, which you know as sure as I do, Scotty. The army don't turn on its own, you know that. Hell, he'll probly get a medal for it. Victories have been hard to come by the last few years."

"Is that what it was? A victory? I guess a celebration is in order."

Bell was slow to answer. When he finally did, he sounded older, beaten down somehow. "You know better'n that, Scotty. But it's never been what happened that counted. It's what folks say happened, what they want to believe. The army knows that, and will tell 'em just what they want to hear. Always been that way and always will be."

"Will you talk to Tim Bledsoe with me? Tell him what happened?"

"What for? I got better things to do than bang my head against a rock I can't break. You want to talk to Bledsoe, you go right ahead. If he asks me what happened, which I know he won't, I'll tell him, but I'm too old for crusading, Scotty. So are you, when you get down to it."

"I'm not talking about a crusade, just about telling the truth to someone who can do something about it."

"We'll see, Scotty, we'll see. Meantime, why

don't you get some rest. You been tore up pretty bad, and it's a long ride on that damned travois."

Horgan closed his eyes again, letting the swaying of the travois lull him. He felt weak and wanted to sleep, but every now and then a particularly hard bounce would send a stabbing pain through his wounded leg, so he couldn't.

He marked time by checking the passage of the sun. After about two hours, he heard the crisp military command to halt, and the horse pulling the travois slowed, then stopped altogether. He heard someone clucking to the animal and turned to see Matt Bell grab the animal by the bridle and tug it. Cottonwoods loomed overhead all of a sudden, and when he twisted around still further, Horgan saw that they had stopped along the bank of a creek.

Bell hitched the horse, then walked over to the wounded man. "Gonna stop for an hour or so, to rest the horses. You want something to eat?"

Horgan shook his head. "Not hungry. Thirsty as hell, though."

Bell nodded. "Be right back." Two minutes later, he approached from the other side, a canteen in his hand. "It ain't real cold, but it'll wet your whistle." He held the canteen out, its lid dangling from a chain, and Horgan wrapped both hands around the cool cloth. The canteen was full, and it spilled over as he tilted it. The water splashed his chest and neck.

It felt good, and he poured a little more on himself, soaking his shirt. Only then did he take a swig, swishing it around for a few moments, then spitting it in a long muddy arc. Trailing behind the horse had covered him with dust, and his face felt like it was covered with mud where the trail dirt and sweat had mingled.

Finally permitting himself a swallow, he felt the water glide down and gave Bell a broad smile. "Better'n whiskey, Matt," he said. "Thanks."

Bell laughed. "You're gonna want a whiskey or two before this is all over. That bullet is still in your leg, and I reckon the doc'll want to cut it out."

Horgan took another mouthful of water. "Harrison got anybody trailing behind us?"

Bell shook his head. "Not as far as I know."

"He around?"

"Up front a ways. You want to talk to him, I'll go get him."

"Yeah, I do. Thanks." He lay back, listening to Bell's heavy steps fade away. He must have drifted off without the steady bounce of the travois to keep him awake, because the next thing he knew, someone was shaking him by the shoulder.

It was Harrison. The lieutenant looked unaccountably happy. "You want to see me, Scotty?" he asked.

"Yeah. I was wondering if you have a couple of men riding on our tail."

Harrison shook his head. "Nope. No need."

"Yes, there is. Those Sioux are not going to walk away from this. They know you have prisoners. And they'll come for them."

"I don't think so. We whipped their tails pretty good. If they're smart, they'll ride the other way if they so much as smell a horse."

"It's not a question of smart, Lieutenant. It's a question of honor."

Harrison snorted. "Honor? Don't try and tell me those savages know the meaning of the word. No sir, they'll steer clear of us, you can bet on it."

"I'm telling you, Harrison, they will come after us. Maybe with reinforcements, if they can round any up. But either way, they'll come."

"Look, Mr. Horgan. You're supposed to be the great expert on wild Indians. Everybody talks about how much you know, how you understand 'em better'n any white man, how you even think like they do. But I have got to tell you, I'm not too much impressed with what I've seen so far. We managed fine so far despite your interference, and I reckon we can manage the rest of the way, too."

Harrison started to move away, but Horgan reached out and grabbed his sleeve. "Listen to me, you fool. We have twenty-five miles of open plains to cross yet. You're going to—"

"Let go of my arm, dammit," Harrison snapped, jerking free. "And don't you ever put a hand on me like that again. You understand me?"

Horgan looked at Bell in desperation. "Matt, talk to him, will you? Talk some sense into him."

Bell shrugged his shoulders. "He's in charge, Scotty. You know that."

"Sheriff Bell seems to understand how things are much better than you do, Mr. Horgan," Harrison sneered.

"You're a horse's ass, Lieutenant," Horgan responded. He struggled to sit up, momentarily forgetting about the ropes holding him on the travois.

Harrison grinned. "Saves me the trouble of clapping you in irons," he said.

"You are going to get more people killed, Harrison. You've already got blood on your hands. You want more, do you? Is that how you plan to climb the ladder, over a pile of dead bodies?"

"I'm just doing my job, Mr. Horgan. No more, and no less. It'd be a hell of a lot easier if you'd cooperate, but since you won't, then I suppose it's just as well you're in no position to interfere. And don't think I've forgotten what happened this morning. It'll get a page all to itself in my report to Colonel Bledsoe. I imagine he'll find it pretty interesting reading. And if I were you, I wouldn't plan on working at Fort Lyon much longer."

"Don't think I'm going to let this go, Harrison. If we survive, I'm going to see to it that you are court-martialed."

Harrison smiled, almost a taunt. For a moment, Horgan thought the young officer was going stick out his tongue and wiggle his fingers in his ears— the look was that spiteful.

Harrison turned smartly then and walked away.

"I should have thought about the trailers, Scotty. I ought to know better. But there's no way in hell he'll do it now, not when he knows it's your idea."

"You know they'll come after us, Matt. Don't you?"

Bell nodded slowly. "Yeah," he said. "I know."

"And you know what will happen to us if they have reinforcements."

"Yeah, I know that, too. I reckon we'll just have to keep our fingers crossed and ask the man upstairs to have a little mercy on us poor fools."

"Might as well ask the village idiot to recite Shakespeare, Matt."

"I guess."

"Look, get me off this thing. I don't want to be trussed up like a side of beef when they come."

"Don't be a fool, Scotty. You can't sit a horse. Not in your condition."

"I can try."

"You'll just slow us down. Better stay there."

"Then give me a weapon."

Bell nodded. "You got it." He stepped forward of the horse, pulled Horgan's Winchester from the boot, and stepped back. Handing the wounded scout the rifle, he said, "I sure as hell hope you don't need to use that thing."

"Me too, Matt."

14

Susan took a canteen and walked over to the old woman, who sat with the three children, two boys and a girl, around her. Her hands were tied in front of her, and they rested in her lap, the gnarled fingers as motionless as a bundle of twigs. One of the children whimpered, and he leaned against the old woman's shoulder.

The wounded warrior leaned against another tree a few yards away, his hands tied behind his back. His shoulder was caked with dried blood, and Susan could see the deep furrow in his upper arm where a bullet had plowed through it. His face was badly bruised, and an ugly knot had risen on his temple where he'd been struck with the stock of a rifle.

Susan unscrewed the cap of the canteen and held it to the old woman's lips. At first, Blue Buffalo Woman refused to part her lips, turning her head away, her face impassive. But Susan persisted. Reaching out to squeeze the leathery cheeks, Susan tried to force the woman's mouth open and, finally, she relented. She drank sparingly, then nodded to the children.

Susan held the canteen out to the whimpering boy, and he looked to Blue Buffalo Woman for permission before wrapping his hands around Susan's and pulling the canteen close. She held it for him while he sucked greedily, water running from both corners of his mouth and trickling down his chest, leaving muddy streaks where the trail dust had been washed away.

When all three children had drunk, she moved to the wounded warrior. He stared at her, his black eyes like two holes bored into his skull. As she held the canteen out, he turned away. Susan persisted, but the captive was adamant. No matter where she held the canteen, he managed to find a way to avoid it.

She heard someone calling her name. At first, she ignored it, concentrating on the job at hand, but when the voice grew louder and more insistent, she turned to see John standing, hands on hips and shaking his head. "Come away from there," he called.

"In a minute."

"Susan, come away," Hansen insisted. "That man's a prisoner."

Susan stood up. "That prisoner's a man," she said. "He's thirsty, and he's hurt."

"That's none of your affair." Hansen took a few tentative steps, then stopped. "Lieutenant Harrison will do whatever needs to be done."

"Lieutenant Harrison is a fool. And he's already

done enough, if you want my opinion," Susan snapped.

Hansen came closer now. "He saved your life."

She shook her head. "No, he didn't."

"But God only knows what would have happened to you, if we hadn't—"

"God wasn't there, John. I was. I know what happened. And I know that it wasn't necessary to attack these people. They were letting me go, John. They were leaving me behind. And Blue Buffalo Woman, too. They were leaving her behind to die."

"Who? What are you talking about?"

Susan stabbed a finger at the old woman. "Blue Buffalo Woman. That's her name. They were leaving her behind. And I told Red Hawk that I would—"

"Who is Red Hawk? Have you lost your senses? What's the matter with you?" Hansen moved back a step, almost as if was beginning to wonder if he knew the woman he was talking to.

Footsteps sounded behind her, and Susan turned to see Burton Fletcher smiling at her. "Sounds to me, Reverend, like the little woman's gone native on you."

"Shut up!" Susan snapped.

"Yep, probably got a taste of lovin' Indian style, and found out she liked it. Most likely that's what happened." He laughed. "How about it, am I right, Mrs. Hansen?"

"You're despicable," Susan said, turning away from him.

"Wouldn't be the first time that happened, Reverend," Fletcher continued. "You know, little lady is used to civilized ways, then finds out there's other ways to do things. Maybe brings a little excitement into her life. She finds out she likes it. Know what I mean?" he winked.

"Don't you talk about my wife that way," Hansen said. "You have no right to say such things."

"Just trying to help, Reverend. She seems pretty fond of that buck over there by the tree. Maybe you ought to ask him for some advice. Hell, you beg him, maybe he'll give you a demonstration. In fact, I—"

Neither of the Hansens had been looking at him, both hoping he would just go away. But when he stopped in mid-sentence, their heads snapped around just in time to see Matt Bell spin Fletcher around and swing from the heels. There was the sharp crack of fist on bone, and Fletcher grunted. He staggered back a step or two, then sat down heavily. Bell strode forward and stood over him. "I told you I didn't want to hear no more out of you, Burt. That's twice, now. Maybe now'll you'll believe me. You'd better, because next time I'm just gonna shoot you."

Fletcher took his chin in hand and worked it back and forth, wincing in pain. "I think you busted my jaw, dammit!"

"Now your mouth works as good as your ears," Bell said. "You leave these people alone or with God as my witness, I'll kill you, Burt." He bent down, grabbed Fletcher by the shoulder and hauled him roughly to his feet. Fletcher tried to pull away, but Bell hung on, grabbed his hand and snapped the arm like a whip, sending

Fletcher whirling around. Then, stepping in close, the sheriff shoved him. "Go on, get out of here before I lose what's left of my temper."

"Was it necessary to hit him, Sheriff?" Hansen asked.

Bell gave him an incredulous look. "No, I guess not, Reverend. I suppose I could have cut his throat. Would you have liked that better, Mr. Hansen?"

"I just meant that violence is—"

"Reverend," Bell interrupted, "violence is a way of life out here. The sooner you, and people like you, understand that, the less of it there'll be. Burt Fletcher ain't worth a fresh horseapple. And if it had been my wife instead of yours, I would have killed him for sure. Now, if you want to go over there and hear some more of his guff, you go right ahead. Be my guest. But I'll be goddamned if I'll listen to any more of it."

He walked over to where Susan stood, and reached out his hand. She gave him the canteen without argument. He squatted down and held it to the wounded Sioux's lips. This time, the prisoner drank.

"What's going to happen to him, Sheriff?" Susan asked.

Without looking around, Bell said, "Well, if Mr. Harrison has his way, and I expect he will, they'll hang him."

"But why?"

"He's an Indian, in case you hadn't noticed, Mrs. Hansen. That's what they do to Indians who have the gall to shoot at white men."

"But white men started it, Sheriff."

"They almost always do, one way or another."

"Can't you stop it?"

"Probably not."

"Will you at least try?"

Bell waited for the Sioux to finish drinking, then straightened up. He handed the canteen to Susan and said, "Mrs. Hansen, I asked for the army's help because you and your damn fool of a husband did something stupid. Now I don't hold that against you, although I know some folks who would. But once I call for the army, the army's in charge. I interfere with that, and the next time some idiot goes off for a walk in the park and gets herself abducted, a snowball in hell'd have a better chance than I would of seeing the U.S. Army. You understand?"

"But—"

"No buts, Mrs. Hansen. Those are the rules. I didn't make them, and I don't have to like them, but I sure as hell have to live by them. So do you." He touched the brim of his hat, and said, "Good afternoon, ma'am." He walked off, leaving Susan to stand with her mouth agape.

John Hansen walked over to her and tried to put an arm around her shoulders, but she turned away. "Don't, John."

"Fletcher was telling the truth, wasn't he? Those Indians, they—"

"Nothing happened, John. Nothing."

"Then why did they take you off like that?"

"I'm not sure. But the time to ask was before the shooting started. Now, it doesn't much matter, does it? I mean, people are dead on both sides and it's our fault."

"No," Hansen argued, "it's not our fault. They didn't have to do . . . I mean, it isn't right. You can't just snatch somebody and carry them off. My God, Susan, they're savages."

"Maybe we could learn something from them, John, if we allowed ourselves to."

"You're talking nonsense. It's they who have to be taught, not us."

Susan spun around to face him then. "Oh, and what is it we have to teach them, how to kill innocent people? How to sneak up in the dark of night and—"

He slapped her so hard her head turned. "Stop it! Stop talking crazy. They might have killed you. What were we supposed to do, let them?"

Once more, the minister tried to put an arm around his wife, and once more she pulled away. "You're upset," he said. "You're not thinking clearly. In a few days, when this is all behind us, you'll understand that we did what had to be done."

Susan shook her head. "No. I'll never understand it." She pointed at Blue Buffalo Woman. "That old woman was going to die. But I said I would take her in, take care of her. They were not going to hurt me. They were *leaving,* John, going away. And they were not taking me with them."

"You were going to take her in? Is that what you said? Are you mad?"

"What was I supposed to do, just leave her there, and let her die?"

"If that's what she wants, then yes. It's not our affair."

"Where's your Christian charity, John? Where is

all that stuff and nonsense about caring for one another, about supporting one another?"

"But she's an Indian, for God's sake."

"She's a human being, John. One of the few I've seen around here lately."

15

They were still twenty miles from Chandler. And Fort Lyon was another twenty-five miles beyond the town. The going was slow, and the sun was beginning to sink when Lieutenant Harrison called a halt to his peculiar column.

Matt Bell moved his horse up alongside the lieutenant's. "What's up?" he asked.

"The horses are pretty well spent, and it'll be dark soon. I think it would be best if we camped for the night and finished the trip in the morning."

"You don't want to camp out in the open like this. Not with Sioux trailing us," Bell said. "It'd be best if we pushed on to Chandler."

Harrison shook his head. "No. It's too far. And the going is too slow. After dark, it'll be slower still. Better to rest overnight."

"Where you figure to hole up, Lieutenant?"

"This is your neck of the woods, Sheriff. You

know someplace close by, someplace with water and enough wood for a fire?"

Bell nodded. "There's a box canyon about a mile east of here. It's got plenty of grass for the horses, fresh water, and firewood ought to be easy enough to come by. There's a stand of big pines. But—"

"Sounds ideal. Lead the way." He wheeled his mount and rode the length of the column, explaining what they were planning to do. When he reached the travois at the end of the column, Scotty Horgan was sleeping, and Harrison didn't bother to wake him.

Matt Bell rode point, and a half hour later, as the bedraggled column reached the crest of a hill, the yawning mouth of Campbell Canyon came into view.

Harrison nodded appreciatively. "Looks like just the thing," he said. "But maybe we ought to go on down and check it out, just to make sure."

Without waiting for an answer, Harrison spurred his horse and plunged over the crest and on down into the broad, grass-filled valley leading toward the mouth of the canyon. Bell had to use the bunched reins to lash his horse to keep up. He glanced over his shoulder and saw the rest of the men beginning to dismount.

When Harrison reached the canyon mouth, he waded his horse through the swift, shallow current of Campbell Creek, then nudged it on through the towering stone walls. Bell followed him through. The walls on either side were over a hundred feet high, and quickly widened away from the mouth in an oblique **V**. The lieutenant walked his mount along the creekbank, turning in the saddle to ask, "How far back does it go, Sheriff?"

"Half a mile. Maybe a little more. Campbell Creek falls into the canyon over the back wall. We can just follow it all the way in."

"The walls this high all the way back?"

Bell nodded. "Pretty much. Haven't been here in a couple years, but I remember it being like a shoebox. Couple hundred yards in, the walls are parallel, run all the way to the back wall. The corners are almost square. You didn't look too close, you'd swear a mason had something to do with it."

"Well, I guess I'll take your word for it. We'll camp under the rear wall. That'll give us some protection. Should be easy enough to defend ourselves here, if we have to. But I don't think we will. Looks to me like Horgan was wrong. There's been no sign of Indians since we left their camp. We put the fear of God into them, for sure."

"Scotty knows his stuff, Lieutenant. I wouldn't be so quick to dismiss what he has to say. I don't know anybody knows more about the Sioux than Scotty does."

"Well, Mr. Horgan and I don't exactly see eye-to-eye, Sheriff. I'm sure you've noticed that." Harrison smiled. "Just as well if I make my own decisions. I'm ultimately responsible, after all. And I don't think it's a good idea to let the command second-guess me. One opinion's about all they can handle at one time."

"It's that kind of attitude gets soldiers killed, Lieutenant. Officers, too."

"I think I know a little more about that than you do, Sheriff."

"I know you do," Bell said, irritated and anxious to conceal it. "You want to go on back and pick your campsite, I'll ride back and get the rest of them."

"Thank you, Sheriff. I'd appreciate it. Make sure they double-time it on in here. I want to be set by sundown."

Harrison nudged his horse into motion again, while Bell turned his own mount, muttering, "I hope to God we see another sunrise, you bull-headed sonofabitch."

The sheriff headed back to the waiting column. He hoped Horgan was awake, and that the two of them would have an opportunity to talk in private. As he rode up the hill, he could see that the waiting men were exhausted. He knew that Horgan was weakened by his loss of blood, and at the moment, he didn't have any idea what to do. But something had to be done, and soon. Harrison was making one foolish mistake after another. Only Horgan knew enough about the Sioux for his word to carry any weight with the lieutenant, but it seemed that Harrison was determined to ignore the scout's advice at all costs, so he was hoping that Horgan would have a few suggestions. If Bell presented them, there was a chance, although slim, that Harrison could be persuaded, after a little arm-twisting, to listen to reason.

Anybody who knew anything about Indian warfare knew that you didn't want to lock yourself in without an avenue of retreat, but that's exactly what Harrison was planning on doing. The sheriff regretted now having mentioned the box canyon. Camping there over night was like gift-wrapping themselves. It might be easy enough to stop the Sioux from getting in, but it was just as easy for the Sioux to keep them from getting out.

And it didn't take a Napoleon to see who would have the easier time getting reinforcements. No one at Fort Lyon knew where they were. And they were far enough from Chandler that it was unlikely anyone in the town would realize their location either.

Which meant that all the Sioux had to do was find another hunting party, at which time the standoff would become a siege. The high walls of the canyon were ideal firing positions, and the Sioux, while not equipped with the best weapons in the world, were probably the best warriors, with the sole exception of the Apache—a distinction, Bell knew, that would be lost on Lieutenant Randolph Harrison.

When he reached the top of the hill, he told Sergeant Anderson where Harrison was waiting for them, and the sergeant rousted his weary charges for the short run to the campsite. Bell hung back, telling Anderson he would take care of Scotty Horgan, give him a few extra minutes of rest before the last leg of the trip.

Bell stood beside his horse, watching the motley band of citizens and soldiers, captives and captors, wind down the gentle slope and start across the valley floor. For a few moments, he actually thought about heading straight on to Chandler. He knew it was the smart thing to do. It might even be the best thing for all concerned. He

could send word to Fort Lyon on his own, and get
Tim Bledsoe to send a relief column.

But Matt Bell had done enough time in blue and
gold to know the book, and its ink still ran thick
in his veins. He would do it the army way, which
meant trying to convince a man who didn't want
to be convinced that he was doing his job badly
and that he'd better straighten up before it got a
lot of people killed. But if his time in the army
had taught Matt Bell one thing, it was that experience was the only teacher, and then only if the
pupil survived the lesson.

Pulling his horse behind him, he walked over
to Horgan's horse. Squatting down beside the
travois, he watched the man sleep for a few
moments. Then, reluctantly, he reached out and
shook Horgan by the shoulder. Horgan's eyes
fluttered, and he mumbled something unintelli-
gible before finally staring at Bell with a slightly
befuddled look.

"How you feeling, Scotty?" Bell asked.

Horgan grinned weakly. "Like I been shot at and
hit, Matt. That's about as close as I can come to
telling you."

"Want something to eat?"

"What have you got?"

"Some jerky is all."

Horgan grinned again. "That stuff'll kill you. I'd
love some."

Bell laughed, then went to his saddlebags and
got three stringy strips of the salty dried meat.
Snatching his canteen from his saddlehorn, he
walked back and sat on the ground beside the
travois. He handed Horgan two of the jerky strips

and started gnawing on the third himself.

"What's on your mind, Matt? You ain't up here for a picnic with an old friend. I may be half-simple, but that's plain as day."

"I dunno. I don't like the idea of spending the night out here so far from help. It's asking for trouble, and we already got enough of that on our plates."

"Spending the night? Whose idea was that?"

"Whose you think it was? I tried to tell him, but he didn't listen. He knows it all, does our young Mr. Harrison. More than you and me put together, I reckon. At least, that's how he sees it. And I for one am tired of arguing with him."

"You want me to talk to him?"

Bell shook his head. "Nope. You tell him anything, he'll go and do the opposite. I wish I could just go on into Chandler and forget about it, but I sent for the help in the first place, and it ain't right to run off now. If something bad is going to happen, then by rights I ought to be there."

Horgan licked his lips, bit off a hunk of the jerky, and didn't answer until he had chewed and swallowed it. "So, what do you have in mind?"

"I was thinking maybe we ought to send a galloper over to Fort Lyon, or at least into Chandler. If we can get some more guns out here, we might be all right. But I ain't quite sure how to get him to listen."

"Just talk to him flat out, man to man. Take him aside and tell him."

"He won't listen."

"Probably not, but at least you'll have the satisfaction of having given it a try."

"That won't save my hair, nor yours either."

"There's worse things. Think of all the money I'll save on combs."

"This ain't no laughing matter, Scotty. There's a handful of people from my town over there have no idea they're standing around watching some idiot whack a hornet's nest with a two-by-four. By the time they realize it, there'll be buzzing from here to the Canadian border. And when you get right down to it, being right ain't no substitute for being alive."

"Do it on your own, then. Just send somebody back. Tell Harrison you got to get a message to your deputy and you have to send a man. I know it's a touchy situation, and it feels like sneakin', but he'll thank you later on. More important, you'll be makin' sure there *is* a later on."

"I'm worried about them prisoners, in case things get ugly. He's likely to take it out on them. I don't much cotton to the idea of bringin' them in in the first place. But if we get our nuts in a bear trap, Harrison might try to make a point with that old woman and them kids."

"I think maybe you're being too hard on him, Matt. He's a fool, but no worse than that."

"I hope you're right."

16

Bell took his time leading the horse and
travois down the slope. It was difficult to
lead the animal and carry on a conversation
with Scotty Horgan, who grew tired of shouting to
make himself heard, so after a couple of
exchanges, both men fell silent.

Bell couldn't shake the feeling that the situation
was explosive, and that Lieutenant Randolph
Harrison was busy fumbling in his pockets, looking for a match. But what Harrison didn't seem to
realize was that he had already lit the fuse that
morning, and it had been sputtering along all day.

Before the night was over, Bell thought, there is
going to be one hell of a big bang. And he hoped
to God that he didn't go up in smoke. He knew
Horgan was sympathetic, but other than the prisoners, the only other ally he might have was
Susan Hansen, and he was anything but certain
about her. She seemed cool, composed, too com-

posed maybe, for what she had been through. Bell had the feeling that she might suddenly run into a wall. And if that happened, she could got to pieces in jig time.

The enormity of Susan Hansen's experience, details aside, could not be overestimated. No one, now matter how courageous, could experience what she had gone through and not be emotionally overwrought. She was likely to come apart at the seams like a cheap suit. It would happen, Bell was convinced, but he didn't know when and he didn't know what it might take to precipitate it. He only knew it was going to happen.

Enlisting her in an effort to control Harrison might be all that was needed to push her over the brink, and if he was going to go eyeball-to-eyeball with the feisty lieutenant, he wanted someone he could count on at his side. Spirit wasn't enough—she would have to *be* there, body and soul. And Bell was anything but enamored of the thought of depending on a minister's wife for that support.

But Scotty Horgan wasn't going to be much use. He knew the scout well enough not to underestimate him. He knew Horgan's strength and the size of his heart. But that strength had been severely sapped, and heart alone would not be enough. Still, the most daunting fact, the one he could not get around no matter how he tried, was that he didn't have the slightest idea of what to do.

Bell was too much of a law-and-order man at heart to pull his Colt and stick it in Harrison's ear. More than likely, it would just get somebody hurt, probably himself, and that wouldn't do the prisoners any good. The troopers were rowdy, as he had been when he had worn the blue and gold, but that didn't mean they would cotton to insubordination on so large a scale, even assuming he could convince them that their lives were at stake. Like all soldiers, they had a kind of fatalism about them, a jaundiced view of the world, and of their place in it, that accepted death at face value. They smiled and thumbed their noses at the grim reaper, mocking his costume and disparaging the edge on his scythe.

On the other hand, turning the prisoners loose to fend for themselves would be worse than cruel. Three children, a wounded man, and an old woman who could barely walk wouldn't stand much of a chance on their own, even if the troopers sat on their hands and watched them walk away, which didn't seem likely.

Convincing Harrison to change his mind seemed like the best course, perhaps the only one that had a chance to succeed. But Harrison seemed to be too caught up in his own narrow concept of military justice. For him, the law had no spirit, was letter only, and at the moment that letter had only one interpreter—Lieutenant Randolph Harrison himself.

By the time Bell reached the bottom of the hill, he was no closer to deciding what to do, and less certain that there was anything he *could* do. He felt paralyzed, and he didn't like it. For a moment, he questioned his own character, accusing himself of being too cowardly to do what any decent man would try to do. But it was much less simple than that, and there was no point in pretending otherwise.

The only avenue open to him was keeping his eyes and ears open for any opportunity to put a bug in Harrison's ear, one that would get his attention without stinging him, one that would make such a nuisance of itself that the lieutenant would choose to rid himself of it on his own.

As they headed toward the mouth of Campbell Canyon, Bell heard Horgan calling to him, and reined in. Dismounting, he walked back to the wounded scout. "You got glasses with you, Matt?" Horgan asked.

"Yeah, why?"

"Get 'em."

Bell nodded, walked back to his own horse, and took the battered case for his binoculars from his saddlebags. Looping the strap for the case over his shoulders on the way back, he squatted down as he handed the glasses to Horgan. "What's the matter? You see something?"

"I'm not sure. I've been half-asleep so long, maybe I'm just dreaming."

"No, Scotty, you ain't dreaming, and we both know it. What did you see?"

"Wait."

Horgan held the binoculars to his eyes, fiddled the focus until it was sharp, then scanned the tree at the top of the hill. He worked from left to right, stopping once or twice, then recovered the same ground in the opposite direction.

"See anything?"

"Nope."

"You ready to tell me what you thought you saw?"

"Looked like two riders. At first, I figured I was

just groggy, maybe imagining it. But the longer I looked, the less sure I was, either way."

"Indians?"

Horgan shook his head slowly. "Never saw them clear enough to tell, but if I had to guess, I'd say yeah, Indians."

"How long were you watching them?"

"Since the last time we stopped, a little longer."

Bell bobbed his head, then snatched a fistful of grass from the ground beside his heels. Tapping a rhythm on his open palm with the bunched grass, he mused, "They know where we are, then, I guess."

Horgan laughed. "Don't tell me you thought they wouldn't know! Jesus, Matt."

"No, I didn't think that. But I didn't figure they'd be on us so soon, either."

"Maybe they're not. Maybe it's just the trackers. There's two of them, so one can go back with the news while the other keeps an eye on us."

"You believe that?"

Horgan was silent for a long moment. "I don't know," he said. "I'm not sure I understand anything anymore, Matt. I feel like I'm getting too old for this bullshit."

"I thought a scout was too old when they put pennies on his eyes."

"I used to think that, too, but now I don't know."

"Well, if I can convince that would-be Tippecanoe back yonder to send a galloper, it won't matter much. We'll have some help before too long."

"If the Sioux don't get the galloper, maybe."

It was Bell's turn to be silent. "They'll get him, won't they?"

Horgan chuckled. "Wouldn't you, in their shoes?"

"If I saw him, I would."

"They'll see him. That's one reason they're here."

"Give me them glasses a minute, would you?" Bell asked.

Horgan handed them over, and watched his friend scan the same terrain he'd just examined twice from horizon to horizon. Bell was humming under his breath while he swept the glasses slowly from left to right. Working his gaze back along the ridgelines, Bell hummed a little louder, something that Horgan thought was supposed to be Foster but that was so off-key it could have been just about anything.

"I don't . . . wait a minute . . . wait just a minute," Bell muttered.

"What is it?"

Bell didn't answer for a bit, and when he did, he said, "Nothing. A deer. I thought it was a pony for a second. But it moved into the light and I could see it better. I don't doubt they're out there somewhere, but I'll be damned if I know for certain where."

He started to get to his feet, slipped, and lost his balance. Grumbling as he got to his knees, he stood up and started toward his horse, then realized he'd left the binoculars on the ground, turned abruptly, and headed back the other way. The whistle of the incoming arrow made him stop again, and his horse bucked when the arrow hit.

From the solid impact and the shrill whinny, he knew the animal had been hit, and he turned to find the arrow to get some idea where it had come from. It had pinned the stirrup to the animal's ribs and was sticking out of the horse's side, right where he'd have been if he hadn't forgotten the binoculars.

Shuddering, the horse went to its knees, and Bell shouted, "Look sharp, Scotty, we took an arrow." The horse gave one more mutter and fell silent. Its body trembled for a few moments, and then it was deathly still.

"You all right, Matt?"

"As it happens." Bell leaned over the horse and snatched his Winchester from the boot, then flopped on the ground beside Horgan's travois. "Sonofabitch nearly nailed me. Killed ol' Curly deader than a doornail, too."

"You better cut me loose, Matt. You can make a run for it on my horse."

"Like hell I will. I leave, you'll be right behind me, Scotty. He's up top somewhere. That arrow came in at a steep angle. Probably arced the bastard long-range. I'd have heard the bowstring, otherwise, too, I think. Keep a sharp eye on the ridge. He cuts loose again, we might spot him. Maybe I can drill him."

"He won't, Matt."

"Why not? He tried once, didn't he?"

"It was a what-if shot. What if I get him, he was thinking. But he didn't, and he knows it, so he'll wait until he gets another good chance."

"You sure about that?"

"I'm sure," Horgan said. "He knows he's too far

away and that you can dodge anything he can chuck at you. He had a rifle, it might be different. But he probably didn't want to waste a bullet. They're too hard to come by, and half of what they got is short-loaded to begin with. And arrows are good at long range like that only if they get you unsuspecting or if they can send in a whole cloud of 'em, so many you can't get away from 'em all. There ain't enough Sioux up there for that, so—"

"Well, then, I reckon I better get my ass in your saddle and haul us both the hell out of here."

Bell went to his dead mount, removed his saddlebags, and draped them over the back of Horgan's saddle. The struts of the travois were lashed through Horgan's stirrups, so he was going to have to ride without their benefit, his legs clamped over the saplings. He wouldn't have much control, and hauling two men and the weight of the travois would slow them considerably. But it beat walking.

Climbing into the saddle, he said, "You keep them glasses ready, and you see an arrow, give a shout. I'll be out of the saddle damn quick."

He nudged the big stallion into a slow trot and headed for the yawning mouth of Campbell Canyon, knowing now that it might not be the only thing to swallow him before the night was over.

Two more arrows sailed overhead as Bell pushed the horse toward the canyon mouth. But both were from long distance, and Scotty Horgan saw them clearly enough to know they posed no threat. The sun was already beginning to set, and the canyon was deep in shadow as the two men drew near the entrance.

Bell didn't stop until they passed through the towering opening. Horgan recognized where they were, and he whistled. "Campbell Canyon!" Turning on the travois, he called, "This is not a good idea, Matt."

Bell reined in and turned to look at Horgan, who was staring up at him, from an awkward angle.

"I know it. But it's too late now."

"No it isn't. We can leave right after sundown. The dark will give us some cover, and it won't slow us down much, because we're not moving that fast to begin with."

"Harrison won't go for it. He's already got his mind made up. No way to make him change it. Not after he's given the order to make camp. It'll make him look bad, and I think he's more worried about that than he is anything else."

Horgan stopped arguing, and Bell slipped from the saddle, landing with a thud that caused Horgan to turn again. "What the hell are you doing?" the scout asked.

"Your horse has been working hard. It isn't far to the back wall, and I figured I'd walk the rest of the way, give him a bit of a rest."

"Wish I worked for you," Horgan laughed. "Seems like it'd be stealing money to collect my pay."

"You'd better save your strength for the run home, wiseacre," Bell laughed. "We're a long way from done with this. Be lucky if we get home at all."

"We'll get home, Matt. It'll take some doing, but we'll make it."

Bell, who wasn't so sure, didn't respond. He grabbed the reins in his right fist and tugged. The horse broke into a walk, and Bell listened to the rasp of the travois poles on the sandy soil as they scraped along. They had gone only a hundred yards when Horgan said, "Uh-oh!"

Bell stopped the horse. "Trouble?"

"You bet it's trouble, Matt. Look back there."

Bell looked at the scout, then followed the direction of his extended arm to the mouth of the canyon. Three Sioux warriors, in full warpaint, sat on restless ponies. They made no move to enter the canyon. They didn't even make any overt sign to indicate they saw the two men, but they didn't have to. Bell knew they wouldn't have been there at all if they didn't know their quarry was penned up like sheep inside the towering walls of the box canyon.

"So much for lighting out after sundown," Bell muttered.

"You can bet they're not alone," Horgan added. "We'd better get our asses to camp and set up some defenses."

"I don't think it much matters," Bell answered. "We're boxed up real good. All we got to do is put a ribbon on the package." He swung back into the saddle, clapping his legs against the exhausted horse's sides, and clucking to him as he jerked the reins. "Giddap, there, come on."

It took five minutes to reach the rear wall of the canyon. A waterfall cascaded down nearly two hundred feet from the rimrock. Its wavering column, catching the light of the setting sun, was brilliant orange. It looked like molten gold scattering sparks as it fell. The dull roar of the cascade's plunge into a deep pool at the base of the wall sounded like distant thunder. A rainbow arced over the pool, shimmering like a snake in the fine mist thrown up by the steady downpour.

Bell saw one of the troopers perched on a rock ledge fifteen feet above the canyon floor, and waved to him. "Where's Lieutenant Harrison?" he shouted.

The trooper pointed. "Over there in the corner, the other side of the pool," he yelled.

Bell nodded his thanks, and turned the tired horse to the left. As he approached the corner, he could hear the sounds of a military camp—the rattle of tin utensils, the nicker of horses, an occasional curse, and the raucous, mocking laughter every soldier was issued with his rifle and canteen.

Bell dismounted and walked to the travois. The soldiers glanced up, then went back to what they were doing. Bell unlashed Horgan from the travois, and the scout sat up. "Feel like a man just reprieved by the governor," he said, laughing.

"How's the leg, Scotty?" Bell asked.

"Hurts like hell. But the bleeding's stopped. I wish we could get the damn bullet out. I'd feel a whole lot better."

"You'd best let a doctor take care of that," Bell said. "You go messing around with your knife, and you're liable to do more harm than good."

"Doctors are only good for telling you what you already know. You don't feel well, and they tell you you're sick. You're realize you're gonna die, and they say you might not make it. Old news, Matt, old news, that's all they're good for."

"Maybe so, but you lost a lot of blood. And that bullet has to come out." He walked into a clump of brush and came back with a stout sapling. Walking over to the campfire, he squatted down, yanked a hatchet out of a short log, and whacked the ends off the sapling, fashioning a makeshift cane. He tossed it to Horgan, who groaned as he got up and put weight on his leg for the first time since being lashed to the travois.

Horgan gritted his teeth, but when he tested the

leg, it seemed to take his weight. "Come on, let's have a little talk with Lieutenant Harrison," he said, limping toward the man in question, who was seated against a fallen rock with John and Susan Hansen.

"This is a good place for a camp, Sheriff," Harrison said, after nodding to the new arrivals.

"I'm not so sure," Bell said.

"Nonsense. It's got everything we need—water, firewood, grass for the horses. It's easy to defend, too."

"How do we get out, Lieutenant?" Horgan asked.

Harrison smiled condescendingly. "We get on our horses and point them toward the mouth of the canyon, Mr. Horgan. How do you think?"

"Do we go over the Sioux or through them?" Horgan asked, grinning back.

Harrison was unruffled. "If there are any, we'll decide in the morning."

"You'd better think on it some right now, Lieutenant," Bell suggested. "Because they're already here."

Harrison lost his control for a second, just a fleeting wash of fear that passed over his face. Like the shadow of a fast-moving cloud, it was gone before anyone saw it clearly, but they all knew it had been there. Harrison, though, tried to sound unconcerned. "You saw some Indians, did you?"

Bell nodded. "Three bucks. Full warpaint."

"Where?"

Horgan jerked his head toward the mouth of the canyon. "They watched us come in. Most likely, they were on our tail most of the afternoon, but they weren't ready to make a move."

"Three, you say? That doesn't sound like much of a threat to me." He laughed, but the sound was forced, and he knew it.

"I said we *saw* three. That doesn't mean that's all there are. They're like ants, Lieutenant. For every one you see, you can bet the farm there's a dozen more."

Harrison was starting to look worried. "What do you think we ought to do, Mr. Horgan?"

He sounded more respectful. Horgan noticed the difference, but didn't call attention to it. They were going to have to work together if they wanted to survive, and Horgan knew it, even if Harrison didn't yet. But he would learn, Horgan thought. He would learn.

"I think," Bell offered, "we better plan for the worst and hope for the best."

"Pretty words, Sheriff. But what do they mean?" Harrison asked. "I can get platitudes enough from the Good Book, but they aren't much help at the moment."

"Soon as it's dark, we'd best try to get a man out, send him to Fort Lyon for help. Right now, we might as well be a thousand miles away, for all they can do. They don't have any idea where we are. We don't know what we're up against, but we can be pretty goddamned sure it'll get worse before it gets better."

Harrison shook his head. "Can't do that. Can't spare a man. We'll need every rifle we have."

"What we need, Lieutenant, is help," Bell insisted. "The only way to get it is to send for it.

It'll be a couple of days, at least, before Tim Bledsoe starts to worry about us. It'll take him another two or three days to find us, if we're lucky. That's five days."

"I can add, Sheriff," Harrison snapped. "But we have food and water. We can stand them off that long. During the daylight, we can keep them away from the rimrock. And Sioux don't like to fight at night, so it should be easy enough to hold our own."

"Who told you Sioux don't fight at night, Lieutenant?" Horgan asked.

Harrison sensed the import of the question and hesitated a moment before answering. "My instructors at West Point."

"Your instructors at West Point . . ." Horgan bobbed his head from side to side, letting his breath out slowly, and sticking the tip of his tongue out between his lips. "Any of them ever see any action against the Sioux, as far as you know?"

"I assume so."

"Well, I assume not, Lieutenant. That's what I assume. Because the Sioux fight whenever they want to, or whenever they have to. If they don't attack us during the night, it'll be because they don't believe they have to. The Sioux don't believe in taking unnecessary risks, Lieutenant. Under ordinary circumstances, night fighting is riskier than daylight combat. But if they think they have to get in here during the dark, they will. Believe me, they will."

"I won't send a man out, Mr. Horgan. We can't spare one. And I wouldn't want to expose him to the risk."

Horgan laughed. "You know what I think, Lieutenant? If things go the way I expect they might, I think that the man you sent would be the lucky one. Maybe the only survivor." He looked at Susan Hansen then, and regretted his bluntness. Her face had gone chalk white.

But she swallowed hard, and leaned forward. "Can't you talk to them, Mr. Horgan?"

"Not now, Mrs. Hansen. The time to talk was this morning. But they've lost women and children now, and they will not be in a talking mood. I can't say as I blame them any, either. Even Red Hawk, who is about as reasonable a man as—"

"Red Hawk?" she blurted. "You know him?"

Horgan nodded.

"What's this?" John Hansen snapped. "You on a first name basis with savages now, Susan? When did this happen?"

Susan shook off his interruption. "Maybe we can—" But the minister grabbed her by the arm and squeezed it hard enough to bring a yelp of pain. "Stop it, John! You're hurting me."

"Let's not squabble among ourselves, folks," Horgan said. "We got enough trouble with the Sioux."

As if to punctuate his words, a single piercing howl drifted down from on high, and Horgan looked up at the rimrock. He saw a solitary warrior, rifle brandished high overhead. Then another appeared, and a third.

Harrison saw them too. "There's your three bucks, Mr. Horgan. Looks like that's all there is."

The words were no sooner out of his mouth

than a fourth appeared, then a fifth and a sixth right behind him.

One by one they appeared, starkly outlined against the darkening blue of the sky. Their warpaint caught the sun and glistened like bands of fire on cheeks and chests. And when the last warrior made his appearance, Horgan had counted fifty-three fully armed men lining the rimrock from end to end.

Now it was just a matter of time.

18

As the sun began to set, one by one, the Sioux backed away from the rim. The clouds turned purple, and bands of brilliant light streamed out from behind them. Finally, only one warrior remained, a rifle held high overhead, the blades of light spearing out around him in every direction. Then, as suddenly as it had started, it was over. The sun went all the way down, and the stars twinkled peacefully over the silence of the canyon. Another howl echoed down among the rocks, muffled by the few cottonwoods along the creek, and then it was still.

"We have to get out of here," Sergeant Anderson muttered.

"We're not going anywhere until morning," Harrison barked. "We're staying right here until daylight. When it's time to move, we'll move, and I'd like to see those damned redskins try and stop us."

142

"They'll do more than try, Lieutenant," Anderson said. "And they won't wait for daybreak, neither."

"I don't want to hear any more from you, Sergeant," Harrison said. His voice was shaky, and Horgan couldn't tell whether it was from fear or rage. "Post sentries. I want four men on alert at all times, three-hour shifts."

Horgan pulled Harrison aside. His leg throbbed painfully as he hobbled away from the others, but he knew that Harrison was balanced precariously on the edge, and that the lieutenant's pride was stretched to the breaking point, his temper along with it. Public humiliation just might push him over the edge.

"What the hell do you want, Mr. Horgan?" Harrison barked, when they were out of earshot of the others.

"There's a few things I think we ought to do."

"Oh, really? Are you in charge here, now?"

Horgan held up a hand to placate him. "No, of course not. You are. But I've been through a little more of this than you have, Lieutenant. We're all in this together, but if we're all going to get out of it together, then we'd all better grab an oar."

"Get to the point, Mr. Horgan. I have things to do." Harrison kicked at the ground, sending stones skittering away in the darkness.

"I don't think we should have a fire. No point in giving the Sioux any more help than we already have."

"Help, what sort of help have we given them?"

Horgan waved a hand. It swept through the darkness in a great circle. "We're in a box canyon, Lieutenant. There's only one way out. Both sides know it. They can starve us out if they want to. The only way we get out of this canyon is if they let us. And you know they won't."

"If you're still arguing for sending someone to Chandler, I already told you that wasn't in the cards, Horgan. Now, unless there's anything else—"

"The fire?"

"What about it?"

"Put it out."

"That's it? That's your accumulated wisdom from twenty years with the noble red man?"

"No. You want wisdom, do you? Here's some. After we put out the fire, I think we should move, scatter around the canyon in small groups. We should keep the horses saddled, and we should try to get out during the night. There'll be a watch on the canyon mouth, but if we try it in small groups, some of us just might get out."

"Turn tail and run, is that your advice?" Harrison spat into the darkness. "You make me sick, Horgan. If we listened to men like you, the redskins would own the whole damned country."

"It used to *be* their country, Lieutenant."

"But not anymore, Mr. Horgan. Not anymore." Harrison turned on his heel. As he stalked off toward the fire, he tossed back over his shoulder, "Don't think I'll forget any of this, Mr. Horgan. Because I won't."

"I'm not worried, Lieutenant," Horgan called after him. "Dead men have short memories."

Hobbling after him, he saw the men clustered around the fire, not close enough that they were directly illuminated, but near enough that their shadowy figures were still visible at some distance. He spotted Matt Bell in the shadows, the only man besides himself who seemed to realize the danger.

"Matt, you better get Mrs. Hansen away from the fire. I don't give a damn if the rest of those fools want to sit there like ducks on a pond, but she's the reason we got into this mess in the first place. Be a shame to come this close, and still lose her."

Bell nodded. "Be right back." Horgan lowered himself to the ground, groaning as he bent his leg before letting it extend out straight in front of him. The pain had lessened somewhat, but he was still weak. He watched as Bell knelt beside Susan Hansen. She was sitting beside her husband, but the man might as well have been a stranger, for all that seemed at that moment to connect them.

Her face seemed slack, almost as if her emotions had been completely drained. She nodded as she listened, but there was a listlessness about her. Bell got to his feet then, and reached down to take her by the hand. John Hansen turned and watched, but said nothing. His face, too, seemed to have gone dead. He was thin to begin with, and yet the flesh of his cheeks seemed to be sagging on the bone. He looked like a skeleton waiting to happen.

Susan Hansen followed Bell into the shadows, her gait unsteady and halting. If he hadn't known better, Horgan would have guessed that she had been injured during the morning's battle. Bell sat beside Horgan, and Susan stood there, looking down at the two men.

It looked to Horgan as if she wanted to say something but either didn't know what to say, or how to begin.

"Why don't you sit down, Mrs. Hansen?" Horgan suggested.

She shook her head, a slow wobble. With the fire behind her, her face was all but invisible. She looked like a dark phantasm, the weight of her buckskin dress rendering her shapeless and indistinct.

"Something on your mind, ma'am?" Horgan asked.

"You have to stop this," she said. "You have to find a way to stop this."

"I'm afraid I'm fresh out of suggestions for Lieutenant Harrison, Mrs. Hansen. He's ignored the best I had to offer. I don't see that he's likely to listen to anything I have to say."

"You have to stop this," she said again, as if he hadn't responded the first time. But this time, she added, "or I'll do it myself."

"I don't reckon there's much anybody can do now, Mrs. Hansen."

"There is! There must be. There has to be. Something."

Before Horgan could respond, the mournful wail of a flute began to drift down from the rimrock high above them. Long, delicate phrases, minor-keyed and plaintive, flowed effortlessly from the wooden flute.

"What in the hell's that?" Bell asked. "Music? Now?"

"Hush. It's absolutely lovely," Susan Hansen said. "Listen."

She turned her face to the dark sky, as if it were the source of the lament. Her head canted to one side, she cupped a hand to her ear, while the other trembled against her hip as if something were trying to get out of her skin.

The wavering tones of the flute cascaded down on them in wave after wave. Phrases echoed off the walls, and soon the song threaded its way among the echoes, the individual strands linking and intersecting, like the strands of a spider's web slowly taking form.

It was nearly ten minutes before the lament faded, falling into the canyon like an unraveling shroud, echo after echo dying away in ghostly trills.

"Siyotanka," Horgan whispered. "That's what the flute is called."

"What was that melody?" Susan asked.

"Death Song."

She stepped back abruptly, almost as if she had been struck. "For us?" Her voice trembled, on the verge of hysteria now.

Horgan shook his head. His voice was hushed when he answered. "No, not for us. It was a lament for a loved one. Somebody up there lost a relative this morning."

Susan hugged her arms to her chest, and her entire body seemed to shiver as if a great chill had suddenly surrounded her. "My God!" she whispered. "My dear God!"

She started to back away, and Bell got to his feet. "Mrs. Hansen, please," he said, "stay away from the light. It's not—"

The gunshot cracked like a bolt of lightning,

and a yelp of pain was all but drowned out by its reverberations. Horgan glanced instinctively toward the fire nearly fifty yards away. He saw a trooper staggering at an oblique angle, two logs on the ground where he had dropped them. He seemed to trip over something no one else could see, and without a sound plunged face forward into the flames.

The explosion of sparks from the sudden crash swirled like fireflies, and several men rushed forward to try and help the wounded man. But Horgan could see that his feet lay still despite the flames swarming around him from the knees up, and knew the man was dead already.

Two troopers grabbed the man by his ankles, cringing away from the scorching heat. Another gunshot cracked, and one of them collapsed in a heap. The other let go of the man in the fire and backed away, turned, and ran. The wounded man now began to crawl away from the fire, and a third shot cracked, the bullet slamming into the earth between his outstretched arms, and he stopped, curling into a ball. Horgan could see the bloodstain high on his shoulder where the first bullet had struck him.

Harrison had begun to shout now, standing at the outer reaches of the firelight, both hands clenched in fists and waving at the rimrock so high above the firelight failed to reach it. It was as if the bullets had come out of the night itself.

"You red bastards!" he screamed. "I'll show you. I'll show you."

"Get him before he gets himself killed, Matt," Horgan shouted. Bell darted forward as Harrison

took two or three halting steps closer to the fire.
The lieutenant was still ranting when Bell
reached him, his voice now raw, his words lost in
their own shrill echoes. It was as if they had blud-
geoned themselves into unrecognizability against
the towering rock walls and had fallen back, broken and bleeding shells, bereft of meaning.

"Lieutenant, don't go out there into the light,"
Bell said, clapping a hand on Harrison's shoulder.
But the lieutenant tore loose and spun around to
face him, his face contorted by rage.

"Those bastards," Harrison screeched, "those
bastards. I'll show them." He turned to his men,
now just jostling shadows in the darkness. "Get
the prisoners and bring them here," he shouted.
"All of them."

"Lieutenant," Bell said, but Harrison ignored
him.

"I want them all here, and I want them here
now."

"Lieutenant, what are you going to do?"

Harrison spun around, his Colt Army revolver
in his fist. "I'll show you. You just watch. I'm
going to teach those red bastards a lesson they'll
never forget."

"Lieutenant, they're innocent people. They're
prisoners of war. They're entitled to—"

"Shut up, Bell, before I shoot you. Just keep out
of my way. You try to stop me, and I'll kill you. I
swear I will."

The troopers hustled the five prisoners into the
clearing, keeping well away from the outer limit
of the firelight. Harrison barked, "Tie them up. All
of them. Tie them together."

The soldiers seemed more afraid of what would happen at Harrison's hands if they refused than what might happen at the hands of the Sioux if they obeyed. They complied, looping a rope around the neck of each of the captives, then fashioning a huge tangle by knotting the five ropes together. The wounded warrior was on his knees, the three children pressing themselves against the old woman.

Susan Hansen took a step forward, then another, her hands held to her face, covering her mouth. Harrison snarled at her, "Stay back, woman." Then, using the Colt as a goad, he prodded the prisoners closer and closer to the fire. The children had begun to wail, and the warrior tried to hold his ground, but Harrison walked over and cracked the butt of the pistol against his skull, knocking him unconscious. Then he grabbed him by an arm and dragged him into the circle of firelight.

He raised the pistol in the air and squeezed the trigger. "Listen to me, you bastards," he shouted, his words bouncing back at him from everywhere. "You want these people, you can have them. Dead! Is that what you want? Is it? Answer me, you red devils! Answer me."

For nearly a minute, there was only silence. It seemed to go on forever. It was broken after an eternity, by a single gunshot. For a few seconds, Harrison spun around like a dervish, trying to pinpoint its location. When he realized where it had come from, his jaw fell open in surprise.

19

Horgan stepped forward, his pistol pointed at Harrison's midsection. "Drop the gun, Lieutenant," he said. He leaned on the makeshift cane and stared at the young officer.

"Are you crazy, Horgan? Do you know what the hell you're doing?"

"Damn right I do. I'm not so sure you can make the same claim. Drop it! I don't want to shoot, but I will if I have to."

"You'll hang for this, Horgan. Mark my words. You'll hang for certain."

"I don't think so, Mister Harrison. Now, I'm going to tell you just once more—drop the gun. You have three seconds."

"You won't get away with this."

"One . . ."

"I swear, Horgan, I'll—"

"Two . . ."

Harrison looked around, as if expecting some-

151

one to come to his defense. But no one made a
move. Slowly, as if his hand were melting in the
heat from the fire, Harrison allowed the gun to
sink toward the ground. It hung for a moment,
pivoting on a fingertip by the trigger guard, and
then it fell to the ground with a dull clink of metal
on stone.

Horgan started to limp forward, but Matt Bell
said, "I'll get it, Scotty." He ran into the light, bent
to retrieve the gun, and when he straightened up,
he tugged Harrison by the sleeve. "Come on,
Lieutenant, get out of the light. You make too
good a target."

Harrison jerked free, and turned to the soldiers.
"Are you going to just stand there and let this
happen to me?" he shouted. "What's wrong with
you men?"

Sergeant Anderson took a step forward, but
Horgan cocked the hammer on his Colt, and
Anderson stopped. Horgan hobbled closer to the
lieutenant. "Sorry, Mister Harrison, but I can't
stand by and watch you do this."

Once more, Harrison turned to his men. "Arrest
him!" he shouted. "Arrest the sonofabitch. Now!"

This time, Anderson made no attempt to move.
He just shook his head and turned away from his
superior, focusing his attention on Horgan
instead.

"Sergeant," Horgan said, "cut the prisoners
loose, would you please."

Anderson started to do as he was told, but
Harrison barked, "Sergeant, you stay right where
you are, unless you want to face a court martial."

Anderson shook his head slowly. "Seems like to

me, Lieutenant, ain't likely any of us'll live long enough for that anyhow."

"You're wrong, mister. I'll see you in the stockade for this. I promise you. This is mutiny. It's treason. And I'll make sure you pay for it."

Anderson shrugged. "Sorry, Lieutenant," he muttered, stepping toward the prisoners.

He grabbed hold of the large knot and started to pry it apart with his fingers. The heavy ropes were stubborn, and it took him several minutes to work the first rope free.

Susan Hansen came out into the light and knelt in front of Blue Buffalo Woman. She tried to comfort the children, who still kept their faces buried against the old woman's dress, sniffling now as the worst of their terror ebbed away.

When the first rope came undone, Susan got to her feet and coiled it in her hands, then untied the noose around Blue Buffalo Woman's neck. One by one, the ropes came free, more quickly now, and as each of the nooses was removed, Susan took the rope and tossed it into the fire, keeping her head turned and trying not to look at the charred remains of the dead trooper.

Each time a heavy coil fell into the blaze, a storm of sparks danced on the heated air and climbed toward the rimrock before winking out high overhead. The stench of hemp was overwhelming now, and Susan held her breath each time she added another rope to the fire.

When all the captives were free, she called for a canteen, and Anderson hurried forward with one in his fist. He handed it to the woman, who knelt beside the unconscious Sioux. Twisting off the cap, she poured water on the man's face and neck, trying to wake him. All of a sudden, John Hansen darted into the circle of firelight and grabbed Susan by the arm. "Come away, Susan. Come away!" he said.

She turned to look at him for a moment. Her expression was so stern, he took a step back. "Come away," he muttered once more.

But Susan turned back to the unconscious warrior, holding his head in both hands and rocking it from side to side. Matt Bell handed her a handkerchief, which she proceeded to moisten, then dabbed at the ugly welt on the side of the Indian's head where Harrison's pistol had struck him.

The man groaned and tried to sit up, but Susan pressed him back. "Don't get up," she said, not sure whether he understood her. But he stopped struggling against the pressure of her hands and lay still, his expressionless black eyes fixed on her face.

"Now what?" Matt Bell said. "You got any ideas, Scotty, or are you makin' this up as you go along?"

Harrison broke free before Horgan could answer, and ran toward Anderson, grabbing hold of him by the shirt front. "Give me your gun, Sergeant," he demanded, grabbing for Anderson's holster and clawing at the flap. Anderson closed his own hand over Harrison's, broke the lieutenant's grasp on his shirt, and held him at arm's length.

"Tie him up, Sergeant," Horgan said. "And gag him, too, if you would."

Anderson looked at the scout uncertainly. "But—"

"Tie him up, Sergeant," Horgan repeated. "I want him under control while we try to sort this mess out."

Anderson called for a rope, and one of the troopers stepped out of the shadows, a coiled rope dangling from one fist. "Maybe we should string him up. As sort of a sacrifice," he suggested. "Maybe they'll let us go, then."

Horgan shook his head. "There'll be none of that. We're doing this by the book from here on out."

John Hansen stepped toward Horgan. He was carrying a rifle, and he raised it slowly. "You're going to get us all killed, Mr. Horgan," he said.

Horgan shook his head in disbelief. "Mr. Hansen," he said, "I'd be much obliged if you pointed that damn rifle somewhere else."

"Did you hear what I said?" Hansen demanded. "You're going to get us all killed." He pointed up at the rimrock, but Horgan didn't bother to follow the extended arm. "I think Lieutenant Harrison knows what he's doing, and I think we should do like he says."

"You do, do you? That's mighty interesting coming, as it does, from a man who didn't have sense enough to carry a gun when he went picnickin' in Sioux country. For your information, Lieutenant Harrison has probably already gotten us all killed. And, just in case you didn't notice, he was about to make an example of innocent people, three of 'em no higher'n my knee. Is that the kind of man you want to make decisions your life depends on?"

"He's a military man. He knows what he's doing. I trust him."

"And you're a preacher, but it doesn't sound to me like you been studying your Bible much lately. You seem mighty eager to take vengeance on somebody never done you any harm. And as I recall the Good Book, vengeance is already spoken for."

"An eye for an eye, Mr. Horgan. That's in the Bible, too."

"I'm with the reverend on this one," somebody shouted from the shadows.

Matt Bell recognized Burt Fletcher's voice. "Burt, this ain't about voting," he said. "Mr. Horgan's in charge now, and he's gonna stay in charge until this is over."

"And I say he's not." Fletcher stepped closer. Bell could see him now, outlined in orange on one side, the other fading to black. Fletcher had a pistol in his hand, and he thumbed back the hammer as he took another step.

"Burt, you been gettin' in my craw all day long. Put down that damn gun and mind your own business before somebody gets hurt."

"I figure this is my business, sure enough. I don't feature standin' around lettin' them redskins draw straws for my hair. Some of the other boys feel the same's I do. I say we vote on it."

"And what exactly is it we're voting on, Burt?" Bell asked. "You want us to decide which of them Sioux gets your scalp? Or are you askin' us to vote on whether or not them kids gets killed for no goddamned reason?"

"They ain't ordinary kids, Sheriff, they're Indians. That's all I need to know."

"Burt," Bell sighed, "It would take a lifetime to tell you half what you need to know. Now, I won't tell you again. Put down that damned gun and butt out."

Bell shook his head, then sighed again, this time loud enough that everyone heard it. He started to move toward Fletcher, but the cowboy backed up a step and raised his gun. His hand was unsteady, and Bell hoped the gun didn't go off accidentally.

Taking another step backward, Fletcher seemed to be crystallizing out of the darkness as more and more of his lanky frame was illuminated by the crackling orange flames. He aimed the gun at Bell, his hand shaking as if the effort of holding the gun at arm's length were too much for him.

The crack of the gunshot took everyone by surprise, especially Burt Fletcher, who was struck by the bullet. He looked down at his chest, then at Bell. "Who done that?" he asked. A bubble of bloody water formed on his lips, and he coughed, then asked "Who killed me?"

He squeezed the trigger of his pistol involuntarily as he started to fall, but the gun had already swept away from Bell, and the bullet slammed harmlessly into the earth at Fletcher's feet. He collapsed on top of the gun and coughed once more, curling his body like a grub.

Susan Hansen covered her ears and screamed. Fletcher turned his eyes in her direction, his lips twisting into something halfway between a smile and a leer. "Ma'am," he whispered. Then he lay still. Horgan limped over to the man's still form and looked down at him. Fletcher was dead, there was no doubt in his mind. And he knew that the shot that killed him had come from up high.

He glanced up at the rimrock. "Red Hawk! I want to talk," he shouted.

His words bounced back at him, hollow, almost mocking in their empty echoes. He waited for an answer, turning halfway around to scan the darkness above him. He was close to the fire's glare now, and not even the silhouette of the rimrock was visible against the dark sky.

Once more the lonely wail of the flute drifted down from on high. And once more, it was the *Death Song*. This time, though, Horgan knew it was not for those who'd died that morning, but for those about to die in the coming assault.

Again, he raised his voice. "Red Hawk! Let's talk."

And again there was no answer. The flute faded away, and the canyon filled with a thick, almost palpable silence.

20

It was apparent that Red Hawk was not going to answer. Horgan's last pleading call died away without a response, and the silence thickened slowly, like water freezing, until the dark ice immobilized everyone in the canyon, captor and captive alike.

Horgan lowered himself to the ground, stretching out his wounded leg to take some of the pressure off it. He felt as if he had failed, as if he had acted too late, and done too little. He didn't know which way to turn. He hadn't been counting on good will from the Sioux, because there was none to be had, and he knew that. Instead, it had simply been a matter of doing what was right, even if the doing had to be its own reward.

Matt Bell sat down beside him. "We're really in deep, aren't we, Scotty?" he asked, leaning back on an elbow.

Horgan just nodded his head.

"Well, I guess I never will get that house or the rocker for the front porch."

Horgan shook his head. "Guess not, Matt. I'm sorry."

"Hell, it ain't your fault. I don't guess I ever really thought I would, anyhow. It ain't nobody's fault, I guess. I can't even work up a real good mad at Harrison, but I need a lightning rod, and he'll have to do, now that Burt Fletcher's gone to his reward, which I suspect will be rather warm. Poor, dumb bastard."

"We have to turn the captives loose, Matt."

"I know."

Horgan tried to get up, using the cane to haul himself to his feet, but his strength deserted him, and Bell got up, then grabbed the scout under both arms and lifted him upright. "God, I feel like an old man," Horgan said. "It don't seem like it ought to be time yet, but I reckon it is."

The canyon might have been empty, except for the subdued mutter of voices in the darkness, where the rescue party had scattered by twos and threes. There were no words, just the intermittent mumble that could have been water from the creek.

"Sergeant Anderson," Horgan called.

"Over here, Mr. Horgan," Anderson answered.

Footsteps approached, and the sergeant's bulky shadow took shape a few yards away. The fire had died down, and the moon had not yet risen, so it was difficult to see him.

"Sergeant, we have to find some way to turn those prisoners loose without getting anybody killed in the process."

"Jesus, Mr. Horgan, I don't know. Seems like to

me they're our hole card. We cut 'em loose, we can pretty much cash in our chips."

"We got no chips to cash in, Sergeant. I think you know that as well as I do. The Sioux are all around us. They will get the prisoners back one way or the other. We might as well let 'em go."

"Maybe we could trade them—" Bell said.

"No, we can't. They know that we're in a box. They also know now that we're not going to harm the prisoners, so we have nothing to give them they can't get for themselves. No, the thing to do is get them all out of here before the shooting starts."

"What about the woman—Mrs. Hansen?" Anderson asked.

Horgan took a deep breath. "That's a tough one, Sergeant, but—"

"Maybe," Bell suggested, "they'll leave her be. She said they were going to turn her loose this morning anyhow. Maybe—"

Horgan interrupted. "That was before we attacked them. All bets are off, now. Whatever their disposition toward Mrs. Hansen this morning, now she's just another white face. And that's nothing to be at the moment."

"Damn it!" Bell muttered. "All these people dead, red and white, and the whole reason it started in the first place was to save a woman who, as it happened, didn't need saving, and now she's gonna end up dead anyhow. It don't make no sense, no sense at all. It don't seem fair, somehow."

"Fair's got nothing to do with it, Matt. Anybody should know that, it's a lawman. Bring the captives here, Sergeant, if you would, please." Horgan sighed, leaned his weight on the cane, and sucked on his lower lip. While he waited, he allowed his eyes to scan the deep black above the canyon, trying to imagine what it would look like when the moon came up, wondering whether he would live long enough to see it happen.

Anderson came back in a couple of minutes. The old woman whimpered in the dark, and Horgan leaned over to pat her on the shoulder. In Lakota, he whispered, "Don't be afraid, grand-mother. Nothing will happen to you."

The children huddled around her, giving her dark bulk the appearance of some strange insect with six tiny legs. The warrior, his hands still tied behind his back, looked on, a brooding presence even in the dark. Horgan moved toward him, a knife in his hand, and when he was close enough, the scout could see the black eyes watching him, aware of the blade but not deigning to pay it any mind, no matter what Horgan's intention might be.

Once more resorting to his fluent Lakota, Horgan said, "I'm going to cut you loose. We are going to let you all go. Make no sound and no one will be hurt. I give you my word this is not a trick. Just be quiet until you are out of the canyon."

The warrior turned and held his hands away from his body while Horgan sliced through the heavy rope. Turning back, he nodded, as if to tell Horgan that he accepted the terms of his release.

"What about us, Mr. Horgan?" a voice asked from the darkness. It was John Hansen, and Horgan groaned inwardly.

"What about you, Mr. Hansen?" he said.

"If you let them go, what happens to us?"

"I don't know."

"I thought you were the great expert on these savages."

"Oh yes, that I am, Mr. Hansen, that I am. A great expert indeed." Horgan laughed bitterly. "But nobody wanted to listen to me when it would have done some good. Now I reckon we'll just have to see what happens, won't we? Maybe we'll all learn a bit from the experience."

Susan Hansen had stood silently, a little apart from her husband, and now she moved forward and spoke for the first time. "What will happen to Blue Buffalo Woman, Mr. Horgan?"

"I'm sure I don't know, ma'am."

"But they were going to leave her behind to die. Red Hawk said that—"

"It's a Sioux matter, Mrs. Hansen."

Horgan turned away from her, and in Lakota told the old woman to keep the children quiet until they were out of the canyon. Then, asking the warrior to lead the way, he told the woman to follow him. Matt Bell said, "You want me to come along, Scotty?"

"Nope! You just stay here and watch my back, if you would, Mr. Bell." Leaning over, Horgan picked up the smallest of the three children, a little girl, and chucked her under the chin. In English, he said, "It'll be all right darlin', don't cry." Then he repeated it in her own language.

Swinging her up to his shoulders, he said, "Hold on," and when he felt her tiny hands encircle his neck, he nodded to the warrior and fell in behind him.

It was a long walk to the mouth of Campbell Canyon, and every step sent a tongue of flame shooting up his hip, but he gritted his teeth and kept on going.

The warrior seemed to be setting a slow pace, in deference to the wounded scout, and Horgan was grateful. It took nearly a half hour, and by the time they reached the canyon mouth, the moon was beginning to rise. Its light speared through the trees beyond, and the shadows gave the walls of the canyon the appearance of coal.

They were almost at the entrance when Horgan heard his name being called, and he turned to look behind him. He could see Susan Hansen outlined against the glittering waters of Campbell Creek.

"Wait," she called. "Please, wait!"

Behind her, John Hansen struggled to keep up with her, and Horgan waited.

When she reached him, she was panting from her sprint, and the minister, even more winded, straggled in behind her.

"What is it, Mrs. Hansen?" Horgan asked.

"I want to go, too. I can't let her die."

"I'm not sure that's a good idea, ma'am."

"What difference does it make? If they're going to kill me, it doesn't matter where. I—"

"Susan," her husband interrupted, "you can't just—"

"John, please, I know what I'm doing. What I have to do. I'm sorry, but I have to go. I promised Blue Buffalo Woman that I would take care of her."

"What about me? You made promises to me, too. What about those promises?"

"The man I made those promises to doesn't exist, John. I understand that now, and I think you do, too."

"But I—"

"John, I'm sorry." She turned away from him then and reached out to take the little girl from Horgan's shoulders. "I can carry her," she said, snuggling the child to her chest.

"You sure you want to do this, Mrs. Hansen?" Horgan asked.

She swallowed hard, then nodded her head. "I'm sure," she said.

"Good luck to you, then."

"And to you."

The minister darted toward her, but Horgan reached out and grabbed him by the arm. "Let her go, Mr. Hansen. Let her go. She has a better chance with them than she does with us."

He stood there, watching them walk between the towering walls of the canyon mouth. The moon was higher in the sky now, its light painting the walls as it climbed. The warrior turned to the left and disappeared and, one by one, those in his wake did the same.

Only then did Horgan let go of Hansen's arm. "Let's go on back, Reverend," he said. He didn't wait for Hansen to answer.

Limping badly from the overexertion, Horgan made his way back to the others. He heard Hansen crunching along behind him, sobbing, and for a moment thought about turning to comfort the minister. But it wasn't his problem, and he had no idea what to say in any case, so he kept his eyes forward and listened to the thud of his cane on the rocky ground. With the moonlight flooding into the canyon now, it was easier to pick his way through the brush and broken rock.

He found Matt Bell and Sergeant Anderson huddled with the rest of the besieged, and Anderson looked at him quizzically. "Well?" he asked.

Horgan nodded, sat down heavily, and lay back, his arms folded behind his head. "It looks like silver," he said.

"What?"

"The canyon—I was wondering what it would look like in the moonlight. It looks like it's made of silver."

"But what happens now?"

"We'll know by sunup, I expect."

"That's it? We just sit here and wait?"

"You got any better idea, Sergeant?"

The flute began again, its tone almost metallic, as if it, too, were made silver by the moonlight. Once more, phrases intertwined with their own echoes, weaving a nearly impenetrable web of sound. Then with one long, mournful wail, the music died away.

A single, lonesome howl split the silence, and Horgan looked up to see a solitary warrior on the rimrock high overhead. One of the soldiers cocked his rifle, but Horgan barked, "No!"

Slowly, almost solemnly, the warrior raised an arrow high overhead, its metal blade catching the moon for a split second, looking almost as if it were on fire. Then, with a sudden jerk, the warrior snapped the arrow in two, tossed the halves over the rimrock and down into the canyon. Horgan watched them fall, all but invisible in the pale light of the moon, and heard them clatter against the rocks at the base of the wall.

When he looked back, the warrior was gone.

"It's over," he whispered. "Finished!"

Bill Dugan is the pseudonym of a full-time writer who lives in upstate New York with his family.

6, 20, 3, 33, 46